Summer
Intern

Also by Carrie Karasyov
& Jill Kargman

———

BITTERSWEET SIXTEEN

SUMMER
INTERN

CARRIE KARASYOV &
JILL KARGMAN

HARPER TEEN

An Imprint of HarperCollins*Publishers*

HarperTeen is an imprint of HarperCollins Publishers.

Summer Intern

Library of Congress Cataloging-in-Publication
Data is available.
ISBN-10: 0-06-115375-3 (trade bdg.)
ISBN-13: 978-0-06-115375-4 (trade bdg.)
ISBN-10: 0-06-115376-1 (lib. bdg.)
ISBN-13: 978-0-06-115376-1 (lib. bdg.)

Typography by Sasha Illingworth
1 2 3 4 5 6 7 8 9 10
❖
First Edition

Acknowledgments

Jill and Carrie thank . . . the amazing
Richard Sinnott, Jennifer Joel, Amanda
Urban, Steven Beer, Tara Weikum, Mary
Miles, Katie Sigelman, and Erica Sussman.

Jill thanks . . . the high school survival
posse: Dana Wallach Jones, Lauren Duff
and Lisa Turvey, plus my cheres Vanessa
Eastman, Jeannie Stern, and Trip Cullman.
Shout-out to the cousin cheerleading
squad: Charlotte and Emily Coch and Julia
and Alexa Kopelman, plus Mom, Dad,
Will, Harry, and the nuggets Sadie and Ivy.

Carrie thanks her family as usual,
the Huitzes and all of the people
who made her past internship
experiences lovely and not so lovely
(which was good fodder for the book).

Chapter One

*I*t was totally surreal: There I was in the midst of a dizzying, glittering collage of designer duds being pushed around on racks by leggy black-clad editors, with a soundtrack of whirring modems, ringing phones, and French accents playing in the background. There were models on go-sees with the bookings department, who were having Polaroids snapped of their gaunt, shiny faces. There were crocodile handbags from Hermès, Valentino, Chanel, and Marc Jacobs being gathered up for a shoot of "Scaley Chic" reptilian accessories. There was an armed guard from Van Cleef & Arpels with a briefcase cuffed to his arm as he transported gems for the "Diamonds Are a Girl's Best Friend" story, and a beret-wearing photographer having a loud fight with the sittings editor about renting out the Central Park Zoo's entire polar bear sanctuary for a ten-page layout of winter's best fur coats.

I was in the frenzied offices of *Skirt* magazine—the top of the top in fashion, pop culture, and beauty; the bible for any aesthete; the cool girl's forecast for what's hot and what to wear, listen to, even eat (i.e., carbs = the devil). It was a kaleidoscopic mix of hipsters, hotties, and badasses, all yapping a mile a minute on teeny cell phones with a stress level you'd more likely expect to see at the Pentagon rather than at Hughes Publications, the mag's parent company. But in the Gehry-architected glass-and-steel offices, the buzz of calamities at deadline was deafening. Like a trunk arriving in St. Bart's with the wrong bikinis. A beauty associate screaming at a makeup artist that the tweezing for the brow story was too arched. A beeper informing a fashion director of a snag in a Missoni dress on location. Drama was all around. And I had just reported for my introductory summer intern meeting in the gleaming glass conference room. I took my place at one of the empty seats, heart pounding. A platter of baked goods and buttered bagels sat untouched as people streamed into the room.

Beside me were my two roommates for the next two months, whom I'd only briefly met earlier that morning: Gabe, a gorgeous androgynous rocker-type with cheekbones one could slash a wrist on, and Teagan, a multiple-pierced Goth gal who was still striking and beautiful despite the sharp objects protruding from her face.

Gabe and Teagan had both arrived a couple of days before me and had already paid a visit to the *Skirt* office. The accessories director had immediately taken them under his wing, filling them in on all the need-to-know gossip.

When the meeting commenced, we were each asked to introduce ourselves. For example: "Gabe Tennant. Sagittarius. Midwesterner. Hung over." My new roomie got some chuckles.

My turn was so yawnsville: Kira Parker from Philly. I'd won the internship through a fashion sketch submission contest sponsored by Cotton, one of *Skirt*'s big advertisers. I was headed to Columbia in the fall. I also blurted out that I was "psyched" to get to know the city, and the second the words came out of my mouth like in a cartoon bubble, I realized I sounded hot off the Greyhound. Oh well. When we were all done, each editor explained which department they headed up, and then Alida Jenkins, the executive editor, took the floor to describe how the intern program worked.

She was ten minutes into her speech, explaining the guidelines of what working at *Skirt* would entail, when the door to the conference room burst open. Standing on the threshold were three extremely well dressed girls, all with different shades of stick-straight long hair (the hair of the one on the left was dark brown with caramel highlights, while the one in the middle possessed the whitest hair outside of a Scandinavian country and the one on the right had the same honey color as Heidi Klum.) They were all clutching Venti-size cups from Starbucks and appeared to have been laughing at some hilarious joke that was so amusing they couldn't stop giggling even when they noticed that the meeting was already in session.

Now me, I would have been mortified to make such a ruckus that every head in the room whipped in my direction, but these girls didn't seem at all fazed.

"Oh my gosh, Alida! Did you start without us?" asked the white blonde in the center. She suddenly looked down at her watch, which I could see from across the room was a solid gold Cartier tank with small diamonds. "Cecilia, you didn't tell me it was ten-fifteen," she said accusingly to the Heidi Klum look-alike. With that watch, who needed their friend to tell her what time it was?

"That's okay, Daphne. Come on in. We're just getting started," said Alida with a tight smile.

"Sooooo sorry, Alida," said the platinum blonde girl. She strode up to Alida and gave her an air kiss on the cheek.

Instead of sitting down, the white blonde—obviously the leader of the pack—turned to face the other ten interns who were seated in the room.

"I'm sure I missed the name game, so I'll introduce myself now. I'm Daphne Hughes, this is my second summer interning here, and I go to Brown." She looked around the room to make sure everyone was paying attention. I moved my eyes to her friends, certain that they would now take the stage, but before they could, Daphne continued. "Listen, I just want to say that I know you all are probably really nervous right now, but don't worry. Everyone is *really* sweet here, and that's why it's the best magazine on the planet, so don't stress. Of course, they'll work us hard, won't they, Alida?"—she didn't pause to let Alida answer—"But it will be so worth it. This is the best way to get your foot in the door if you want to have a career in the fashion world."

This girl was gutsy. What she had said was basically neutral, but it was the way she said it that was sort of, I don't know, offensive. She was so confident. And patronizing. It was as if she owned the place.

"So, now I'll hand it over to you, Alida, but let me also introduce my friends, because they hate public speaking. This is Cecilia Barney," she said, motioning to Heidi Klum's clone, "and this is Jane St. John," she said, pointing to the brunette.

Both girls lowered their eyes and smiled slightly. "Say hello!" commanded Daphne.

Her friends mumbled something and Daphne smiled as if to say "these guys," and then they all walked to the front row and sat down.

"Okay, so let's continue," said Alida.

The rest of the meeting progressed and Alida explained protocol, rules, safety, and everything else. I listened attentively, but every once in a while my eyes were drawn to the backs of Daphne,

5

Cecilia, and Jane. Just their posture seemed intimidating.

Finally, the meeting was wrapping up, and Alida took on a serious tone. "Lastly, I want to say that you will all be assigned to different editors by the end of the day. Once you get your editor, there can be no trading, unless the editor requests a change. But there is one position that will not be decided today, and that is the most coveted one: assistant to Genevieve West, the editor in chief." Alida said Genevieve's name with reverence. "That will be rewarded in two weeks' time and based on performance. It is a demanding job, and only *one* of you will get it. Even though it's challenging, no one will get an education like the one they get under Genevieve's tutelage. So I suggest you all work hard at your various posts, because that is the only way you have a chance at working in the editor in chief's office."

I knew then and there that I had to have that internship with Genevieve. That would be like the apex for me. I planned to bust my butt over the next few weeks, take additional assignments, offer to help anyone, and do whatever was needed to get that job.

Daphne raised her hand and Alida nodded. "Last year Genevieve had *two* interns—why not this year?" asked Daphne petulantly.

"She thought it got a little hectic, all the people in her office," said Alida.

"She's such a nut," said Daphne with obvious fondness. "Okay, girlies," she said, rising and signaling to her friends. Then they all stood up.

Alida seemed surprised slash annoyed that Daphne had called

an end to the meeting but didn't say anything and instead stood up also. "The sign-up for which editor you want to work for is over here," she said, motioning to the corner.

Daphne and her friends continued walking out of the room. "I'm working for *you* again, Alides," said Daphne with a smile. "And put Cecilia down with Richard and Jane down with Stephanie," she said, more of a command than a request.

Alida nodded, her brow furrowed. It was obvious that Alida was not psyched for Daphne to work for her again.

As soon as Daphne and her gaggle left, everyone else seemed to exhale and ran over to the sign-up sheet. Did they have some sort of prior knowledge of who was nice and who wasn't? 'Cause I sure didn't.

"Who are you going for?" I asked Gabe.

"I put myself down for Warren Frank. He's a queen, too, and brilliant with photographers. I heard he's a bit of a diva, but I think I can handle it," said Gabe.

"What about you?" I asked Teagan.

"Slim pickings, but Viv Mercer, the sittings editor."

I glanced at the list. All that was left was CeCe Ward, the bookings editor who was supposed to be the devil, or someone named Mary-Elizabeth Fillerton, who worked in fact-checking. I didn't want to spend the entire summer stuck in some room surfing the net to find out what year Cindy Crawford and Richard Gere divorced or other boring stuff like that, so I took a deep breath and wrote my name down next to CeCe's. I prayed that rumors of her nefarious exploits were exaggerated. But it didn't matter, anyway, because I planned on working there for only two weeks before I made my move to the editor in chief's office.

When I noticed everyone had left the room, I leaned into Gabe and Teagan.

"So what was the deal with that girl Daphne? She seemed to think she, like, *owns* the place," I joked.

"Sweetie, she *does* own the place! Didn't you hear her last name?" asked Gabe.

"I don't remember."

"Hughes. As in Mortimer Hughes. As in her daddy is our boss's boss's boss, the big kahuna," said Gabe.

I took a deep breath. Ahhh, now I got it. Wow. No wonder she was so bossy. And confident. I guess billions'll do that.

Chapter Two

*A*fter the meetings, we were divided into groups for our office tour. I stuck with Gabe and Teagan, trying to Xerox each person with my eyes, cataloging them one by one into a mental face book. Despite her five-inch Manolo Blahnik stilettos, Alida had a fiery-quick pace that was hard to keep up with in my studded ballet flats. I trailed her through the circuitous route around the high-ceilinged fashion zone as she gave us the lay of the land, like the bar scene in *Goodfellas*, minus the guns.

Gabe leaned in to whisper a hilarious running commentary, which had me in stitches. A crazy-looking woman stormed through the hall on her cell phone, ranting to Air France about lost luggage.

"That's your boss, CeCe Ward, the model bookings editor," he said, wincing. My heart suddenly sank. "The rumor is if you bring her a latte with one percent milk instead of skim, she'll not only throw it at you but also puke up the forbidden sips she already swallowed," he testified.

"Shut up!" I marveled incredulously. And horrified.

"Oh yeah," added Teagan. "She supposedly fainted at Fashion Week backstage at Galliano 'cause she'd eaten one croissant flake in three days."

I knew this world would be obsessed with image, but that was too much. I was in for it with this CeCe person.

"This is the photo department," Alida said, pointing to a sunlight-filled studio with drafting tables and loops to study negatives from recent shoots.

"Pardon me," said a voice behind us, interrupting my fascination with the flawless view of the Hudson River through the photo department's panoramic window. I turned to find the most gorgeous guy carrying about five black briefcases. He was tall and thin, with brown hair and enormous caramel eyes flanked by the thickest eyelashes I had ever seen.

"So sorry, it's portfolio drop-off today," he added, smiling as he lugged the piles of slick portfolios over to a corner drafting table. He walked back to where we stood in the arched doorway. "Hey, sorry about busting by there. I'm James."

He reached out to shake my hand, and before I even blurted

out "Kira" I spied Gabe and Teagan nudge each other and smile. Alida had already moved on for the rest of the tour, and we hurried to catch up. We weren't seven steps away when Gabe launched.

"Honaaaay, you were blu-shing! Is he a *scorcher* or what?" he razzed. "James Carlson. We met him yesterday and I almost collapsed. I mean, I almost needed a defibrillator like in *ER*. He's the photo assistant editor. He went to Brown, and is Zeus come down from Mount Olympus. I mean, bring me *that* on toast points for breakfast any day."

Shoot, I was blushing. My darn face always belied every emotion with a color—green for sick, yellow for tired, blue for cold, and red hot for the heat of embarrassment. "He is cute," I admitted sheepishly.

"And, drumroll—" said Teagan, winking at Gabe. "He's straight. Sorry, Gabe, he doesn't play for your team, my sweet."

"Alas," mooned Gabe. "Thy speaketh the truth. He is as straight as the new Armani pencil skirts for fall."

We arrived in a corner section of the office that looked a lot less glamorous than the labyrinthine lanes we'd walked to get there. There was a bullpen of cubicles, each with a phone and computer. Gabe and Teagan plopped down at their desks and showed me my station next to them.

"The Trumpettes got the best desks by the windows, naturally," sneered Teagan.

"Big shocker," added Gabe.

"The *who*?" I inquired.

"The Trumpettes. You know, Daphne and her gang. It's the

clique of heiresses who get jobs here every summer 'cause Daddy's an advertiser or BFFs with Genevieve West—the editor in chief—or someone megawatt," Gabe explained. "Band of beeyotches."

"They all roll on in leisurely at like ten-fifteen on their studded cells with blown-dry locks. Total brats on parade," said Teagan, rolling her eyes. "A bunch of years back, Cartier Trump had the gig thanks to her billionaire pop, and the name for their gaggle stuck."

"How'd you learn all this stuff in one day?" I asked. Just then, the answer came around the corner.

"Hiiiiii, orphans!" squealed a gray-haired guy wearing a neck scarf and motorcycle boots. Someone actually topped Gabe in over-the-topness.

"Oh, you're cute. You are rocking that belt," he said, looking me over. "Richard Finn, accessories director."

"Richard is the eyes and ears of this institution, like the janitor in *Sixteen Candles*," Teagan said, "but without the broom. He filled us in on *everything* yesterday."

"Oh, I got your broom right here!" he said, patting his pants. I laughed, blushing again.

"So, Kira, right? Aiiight, baby, we're gonna throw you to the wolves today, baptism by fire, best way to learn."

Gulp. I just hoped I wouldn't get burned.

As Richard walked away, we all bemoaned the fact that we were not going to be working for someone like him.

"It's so effing unfair that those little heiresses can pick and choose who they want to work for," lamented Teagan. "What a bummer that Daphne Hughes's mute idiotic friend got Richard for a boss!"

"I know. It would have been the best. He seems so nice. And so is Alida," I added.

"They know who is nice and who is mean. That's why they snag all the good spots," said Gabe.

"And do no work," said Teagan. "We heard they take two-hour lunches, which cost more than the editors make in a week, and then bail early to get 'manis'!" she mocked with finger air quotes.

I was neither a wealthy socialite who could call my own shots at *Skirt* nor a punkish rule breaker determined to make a statement, like Gabe and Teagan seemed to be. I guess I was somewhere in between. I had always thought I had killer style—in school, when all the girls in my class took to wearing exactly the same outfits that Jessica Simpson and Nicole Richie were wearing on the opposite coast, I didn't let that influence me. I scavenged flea markets and vintage shops, raiding my great-aunt Mimi's closet (she was something in her day, according to her, anyway), and put together a look that I felt was distinctly me. This was no Sienna Miller copying Kate Moss situation. I had my own thing goin' on. My friends, while telling me I looked cool, all admitted that they would never have the nerve to wear the clothes that I did. Translation: Some of my stuff is semi-weird. Leg warmers in April? Vests over T-shirts? True, it all sounds pretty heinous when you dissect it like that, but the overall effect was pretty chicadelic, I swear. I felt that my fashion style is what separated me from the crowd, allowed me to express my individuality and all that new-agey stuff. (Paging Dr. Phil.)

But that all came to a screeching halt last night when I arrived in New York and headed for my hotel, where I'd stayed for a night before moving into the apartment I'd share with Gabe and Teagan. When my taxi pulled off the FDR Drive into the East Village and I glanced out the window at the people on the street, I was shocked. I was—gulp—not that original. Those leg warmers that I thought so chic and unusual? I saw four people wearing them in a one-block radius. And I guess vests weren't my reinvention, 'cause I spotted a gaggle of girls prancing around in them. Yikes. Was my eclectic-style persona fading away? Was I just not that interesting anymore? Maybe what was edgy in Philly was not so slick in the grit-filled Big Apple. It started to slowly dawn on me that this was New York—Manhattan—and what was inno-vative in Philly was totally common here.

Suddenly, as I sat there at that cubicle, the summer seemed like it would be very long and lonely. Would I become friends with any of these people? Or was I going to be hanging solo, counting the days until it was all over? I didn't know. But out of nowhere, the face of James, the guy from the photo department, came into my mind. He was hot, and he definitely seemed nice. Maybe he and I would be friends. Maybe more. And before I knew it, my mind was racing with thoughts of James and me dining at sidewalk cafés and going to see Woody Allen movies at small alternative theaters. But okay, full disclosure. I am a pretty confident girl, not cocky or arrogant. I have always aced school, had a sense of self and strength to conquer whatever I put my mind to—except maybe when it comes to the opposite sex. I kind of still haven't mastered that one, and am often confounded as to what drives these beings, or how we're supposed to relate to them. Sure, I've dated, had a boyfriend or two, but I've never yet really connected to any of them.

"Yoo hoo, earth to Kira?" Gabe's voice interrupted my glum reverie of solitude.

"Sorry," I said quickly.

"We've got to go report for duty. You coming?" he asked.

"Yeah," I said, following him and Teagan.

We walked down a long hallway, turned a corner by the Xeroxes, and were suddenly face-to-face with Daphne and James. Huddled together. Intimately.

"Hey," said James.

"Hi," we all mumbled.

Daphne just looked at us from top to bottom, smiled, and said nothing.

We kept walking. When we were out of earshot, Teagan leaned over and whispered to me, "I forgot to tell you, I overheard an editor talking in the bathroom. Hot James? He's Daphne's *boyfriend*."

Good thing she was in front of me and didn't see my face turn purple. I winced as my flickering Manhattan montage of courtship faded to black.

Chapter Three

"And you are . . . ?" asked the ice-cold voice as I lingered nervously in the door frame.

"Kira. Your intern. For the summer," I replied, shuffling back and forth like a three-year-old who had to pee.

"Ugh, I always forget what day you people start," she said, rolling her eyes. "I swear, sometimes this intern program is more trouble than it's worth!"

Was it too late to switch to boring fact-checking?

"S-s-sorry" was my tepid response.

"We are a *magazine*, not a forum for education!" she huffed. "But no matter. Maybe one day you'll be running this place!"

I smiled hopefully.

"HAHAHAHAHAHAHA," she wailed in piercing hyenalike laughter, her head thrown back. I guess she had been joking.

"Have a seat," CeCe Ward finally said, looking me over and gesturing to an extremely uncomfortable-looking steel stool. Behind CeCe was a wall of model cards, five-by-seven-inch glossies with sexily posed women featuring their agencies' logos in the lower-right-hand corner: Ford. Wilhelmina. Elite. The models' names were in bold in the lower-left-hand corner: Esmé. Lila. Eugenia. Zxykasmir.

Face after beautiful face, the girls were at the top of their game, booked in the editorial pages of *Skirt* to be shot by the best photographers in the world. And all day, and often into the night, CeCe Ward had to stare at them. No wonder she was bitter.

"All right, you can start by sorting the new model cards," said CeCe with a sneer. She opened her crocodile Hermès Kelly bag and unzipped a compartment, retrieving cigarettes. She put a finger to her lips as if to say "shhh" and lit up. I knew smoking was strictly against the rules, but I had no choice except to sit in her clouds of smoke while sorting the cards into piles: blondes, brunettes, redheads, and parts models—for when we did shoots of just legs for shoes or hands for rings, etc.

"Is it true there's some butt model who makes like fifty grand a shoot?" I asked, trying to make conversation as CeCe puffed away.

"What's that expression they have in Europe? Children are to be seen, not heard," she sneered. "It's like that here." She patted my head and walked out, extinguishing her Satan stick in an ashtray right next to me. Great. So much for my big learning experience. I was starting to think my summer was turning out to be a wash. I had walked away from making thousands folding shirts at Anthropologie in Philly to making zero in New York at this unpaid internship while being treated like a zero at the same time.

After opening two hundred something envelopes, I was elated that the lunch hour was upon us. There was usually so much work that Gabe had been told no one really left for lunch except the Trumpettes, and that the food was cheap and low-cal in Hughes Hall, the cafeteria for Hughes Publications.

The all-glass dining hall was like something out of *Star Trek*—podlike sitting areas encased in glass for privacy so groups could have private convos while their fabulous clothes were on display. The aisles were like catwalks with beneath-the-floor lighting, rendering them mini-runways for the beautiful people to stroll en route to sitting down with their salad.

My friend Cassie and I always used to joke about what a nightmare it would be to slip and fall during lunch in our high school caf. But in retrospect, a tumble like that in front of dumb jocks and pom-pom toters was little league. To take a spill here and wipe out in front of everyone—now *that* would be horrifying beyond words.

Gabe and Teagan got gourmet salad bar spreads while I waited in the quesadilla line. When I finally got the goods, I nervously walked down the lit aisle and surveyed the scene, spotting my roommates in a pod by the window.

"Hi, guys," I said, overwhelmed. "This place is crazy."

"I know, sticks on parade, right?" joked Teagan.

"Hey, whores!" laughed Richard, who came over with a liter-size Diet Coke. "I'm plopping with you for a sec. How ya holding up, new girl?" he asked me. "Is CeCe a freak or what? She's living proof that not all the nuts are in the nuthouse."

I smiled, and before I could give a response, James came waltzing over.

"Hey, guys, can I crash your table? Our whole staff seemed to go out today. Nothing like bailing when we're on deadline," he said, shaking his head.

"Where's the Dapher?" Richard probed.

"Out with Jane and Cecilia, at some new Ian Schrager hotel café."

"Oooh, you mean C-Level? The one with the ginormous fish tanks with merpeople swimming in them? Awesome!" gushed Gabe. "I just read in *The Village Voice* that it takes like two months to get in there."

I labored with my plastic knife and fork to get a soggy bite of quesadilla and not look like a total slob, all the while imagining Daphne and her clones delicately wielding custom chopsticks to pluck a perfectly rolled piece of sushi off some merman's ripped abs.

"So how are you guys doing?" asked James. "Kira, you're with CeCe, right? How's that been so far?"

19

Heavens open, clouds part, angels sing their soprano chorus: He remembered my name! *And* who I worked for. I was officially on the radar. Wait—Kira, you effing idiot. He's *with* the billionaire pixie owner of the pod, the caf, and the building you're sitting in! The flaxen-haired nymph who dines not at Daddy's dumb caf for worker bee drones but at the hardest place to book a table in the city! Pull the rip cord on the parachute back to earth.

"She's . . . something" was all I could lamely muster.

"Her intern hazings are fabled," James said, laughing. "But I bet you can handle it," he added with a warm smile.

"I hope." I shrugged. "I'd be psyched for the Genevieve West gig, though. I think I'm going to toss my hat in the ring for that."

"You go, girl!" said Richard, patting me on the back. "Go for it! Why not?"

Gabe and Teagan were quiet. Uh-oh. Things could get really dicey if we had to go head-to-head for the internship. But I had no choice. I was here to learn as much as possible, and it's not like Gabe and Teagan were my best friends from childhood. I took a deep breath.

"Are you guys trying out for it?" I asked, trying to be casual. "I just figured you're really in the thick of it then and could learn a ton. I don't know . . . I probably don't have a shot but—"

"I'm not trying," said Gabe. "I love Warren, anyway."

"Me, neither," added Teagan.

My body relaxed. It was terrible but I was glad that there were two down, which meant less competition for me.

20

"Plus . . ." Teagan continued, looking at James carefully. "It's kind of stiff competition."

I stared at Teagan, who locked eyes with me, and I knew what she was saying in the unspoken subtitles: Teagan did not want to mess with the boss's daughter. Clearly, Daphne was the queen bee—even Alida walked on broken glass around her—so no way would Teagan or Gabe rock that boat. Or should I say yacht. No matter how hard I worked, no matter how little Daphne did, everyone assumed she'd get the job. That was how it worked.

I was suddenly getting the picture: Daphne Hughes got anything and everything she wanted. Whenever she wanted it. But you know what? Not this time. No way. I wanted that internship, and I was going to get it.

Chapter Four

*A*fter work, Gabe and Teagan took me to our pad down-town. Because I'd found out I'd won the internship just last week, I'd had little time to prep for the move. I'd decided to spend my first night in a hotel to rest up for day one, so I was just now seeing my summer abode. For some insane reason, I was envisioning the set of *Friends* or one of the funky lofts on *The Real World,* complete with state-o'-the-art electronics and hotties shooting pool on our living room billiards table. My daydream couldn't have possibly been more off base. But hey, if those shows were actually the *real* real world, the cribs would be tiny, grody hovels, just like *our* summer apartment. Gabe and Teagan had settled in and already claimed rooms. So, naturally, I ended up with the smallest, which was literally no bigger than a closet. With no closet in it, my stuff would hang on a rack in the hallway. Good times. Next to my army-style cot was a teeny side table with two drawers for all my stuff. Bonjour, Alcatraz.

After unpacking I plopped in the living room, which looked like Pier 1 had exploded. Gabe suggested we hit Schiller's, a restaurant that he'd heard about from one of his friends. The food was really good and the atmosphere cool, but I wasn't sure I would be able to afford eating out like that every night. Or even every week. Maybe once a month. I was glad, though, that I had a chance to get to know Gabe and Teagan better. Well, Gabe anyway. Teagan was really private and said very little about herself, and usually used sarcasm to answer any serious question. All my efforts to penetrate were deflected. She was totally cool about filling us in on what she had heard about the magazine from a friend who worked there last year, but when it came to personal stuff, she was mute.

Gabe, on the other hand, let everything just flow without an edit button. I could tell he was the type who liked to use his friends as psychiatrists. He explained that he was from the Midwest and his parents were really conservative Catholic Italians who had no idea he was gay and would freak if they did. He had two brothers and two sisters (and had always loved doing their hair and picking out their outfits), and they were totally loving, but he always pretended to be into sports and stuff when his dad was around. The big secret was that his parents thought he was going to the University of Wisconsin this fall and had no idea that he had accepted a full scholarship to Parson's. In fact, they thought he was interning this summer for *Sports Today,* one of Hughes Publications' other magazines. He planned on coming out to them and telling them about school at the end of the summer, and was prepared for a huge meltdown. I said I would stand by with Kleenex and defibrillators.

When we got home at midnight, I was so exhausted I thought I'd pass out—on my cot that looked like a house party for bedbugs.

Teagan ran a black-nail-polished hand through her raven hair. "Kira, I feel bad you got the shittiest room. If you wanna trade halfway—"

"Oh, no, it's okay," I said truthfully, touched by her offer.

"I'm so wiped out, you guys, I'm hitting the hay," Gabe moaned. "I can't believe I'm dying for the weekend already and it's only Monday night."

I felt the same way. Especially because I had the sinking feeling that the long days working beside CeCe could be measured in dog years.

The next day, I was on my knees, attempting to alphabetize back issues of Russian *Vogue* (which was virtually impossible considering I can't read Cyrillic), while I listened to CeCe dissect yet another fifteen-year-old wannabe model to her face. It was amazing how she could be so cold, and equally amazing that these girls would sit there and take it. I'm sure the second they were out of the room they burst into tears, but before they did, they were somehow able to sit there stoically and listen to an evil woman not half as pretty as they were go on about how they were too fat, their nose protruded, their look was too eighties, their hair too long, their eyebrows too arched, their ankles too thick, and so on and so on. From my angle on the floor, CeCe's desk obstructed my view, but I could hear everything. She criticized one girl so severely that simply listening you'd think she'd be a zit-covered walrus, but when I looked up I saw a dangerously thin redhead with a perfect oval face, porcelain skin, and china blue eyes that were filling up with tears. Forget *Skirt*, CeCe should be interrogating prisoners at Guantanamo Bay.

The door opened and closed again, and I stopped to rub my temples. It was only eleven o'clock but I was already beat. "Hi, CeCe," said a voice that belonged to someone wearing lizard-skin Jimmy Choos.

I was waiting for a cold, terse reply from CeCe but was shocked when she warmly said, "Hiiii, sweetness!"

Was this one of her favorite models? Oh God, what if it was someone like Gisele? Or Natalia Vodianova? But the voice didn't have an accent. Maybe it was Christy Turlington stopping by for old times' sake?

"I am so beat," said the voice, and flopped onto a chair.

"I hear you," said CeCe sympathetically.

"Can I have a cigarette?"

"Sure."

Must be another editor, I thought. I returned to shuffling the magazines around.

"Wait, is someone in here?"

Suddenly a face appeared under the desk. As her head was upside down, it took a second to recognize the small cornflower blue eyes and slightly weak jaw with the overly plump pink lips to compensate.

"Hi, Daphne," I said.

Daphne flipped her head back up. "CeCe, what's your intern doing on the floor?" Daphne laughed. "You are so mean!"

CeCe laughed and looked down at me from her desk chair. "She doesn't mind. You don't mind, right?" she asked, not waiting for an answer.

I stood up. "I'm organizing CeCe's magazines."

Daphne looked me up and down from head to toe. I was glad I had taken extra time to dress this morning, choosing a vintage eyelet skirt that was summery and a bit formal, and I had accessorized with a big belt and some wooden necklaces to make it casual. I could tell Daphne approved. She in turn was wearing size zero peach pedal pushers with a chic white blouse tucked in. She definitely went for the preppy, rich Southampton look. I watched her face and saw that she didn't know how to respond, but suddenly she stuck out her hand.

"We haven't met yet. I'm Daphne Hughes." She liked to

include Hughes. I've heard of some boss's daughters going incognito so they could get down with the people, but Daphne was having none of that.

"Kira Parker."

"Where are you from, Kira?" she asked.

"Philadelphia," I said.

"Suburb or the city?" she asked.

"Right outside. Bryn Mawr," I said, looking her carefully in the eye. I sensed that she liked to interrogate people and used it to get them to bend, but I wasn't game for that.

"Are you in college?"

"Going to Columbia in the fall."

"Good school. Ivy. I go to Brown," she said, running her hand through her hair.

"I know. You mentioned that at the meeting."

"Right," she said, momentarily confounded. "What brings you to *Skirt*?" she asked more boldly.

"Cotton," I said.

Suddenly she laughed. "That's a funny way to put it. You won the Cotton internship?" she asked.

"No, my papa has a plantation. He did well this year, so I could afford to come to the big city," I said. She looked confused and then I smiled. "Yes, I won the internship."

I could tell she wasn't used to being teased because she was suddenly finished with me and turned her attention back to CeCe. "CeCe, I wanted to ask if you could call your friend Mickey and ask him to put me and my girls on the VIP list again for Butter tonight. Getting in shouldn't be a problem normally, but last night Jane threw up on Tobey. It was a total accident but they made a big deal about it, and so we're kind of like banned for a week, which is so ridick, so could you call Mickster for moi? The VIP list should take care of things," chirped Daphne.

"That should not be a problem," said CeCe, like a soldier following a commanding officer's orders.

Since my conversation with Daphne was over, I sat back down and continued cataloging. But Daphne then addressed me again.

"You are so lucky to be working with CeCe. This is the best job in the place," she said with a fake smile. Oh yeah? Then why didn't *she* want it?

"I tell her that, but she's already told me she's going to try to go for the internship with Genevieve," said CeCe, waving her cigarette in the air as if this were the dumbest thing ever.

Daphne laughed and her eyes narrowed. "Well, don't get your heart set on it," said Daphne. Her voice was different this time. It was more of an order than helpful advice. Whatever. Now that she knew I had thrown my hat in the ring, let her try to compete with me. I can be a pretty good foe, if I do say so myself.

"She's got a shot, Daph," said CeCe. "Remember that Genevieve likes to toy with your father, show him who's boss. She didn't even let your stepsister get the job in her office, and Saskia made it known that it was the only place she wanted to work."

Daphne's face turned dark. "Well, Saskia is a fool, so I don't blame Genevieve for dissing her. But Genny and I are dear friends. Many a fashion show we've spent huddled together trashing the idiotic celebrities in the front row. No way will she pick someone else over me."

Daphne turned and glared at me to make sure I heard her.

"You're probably right," said CeCe, backing off.

"Anyway," said Daphne, stubbing out her cigarette. "I should get back. There's a sample sale at Chanel today and I don't want to miss it. They said I could come extra early to peruse the goods before anyone else."

"Lucky girl," said CeCe.

Why the hell did she need to go to a sample sale when she could buy anything at full price? That didn't seem fair.

"Bye, Kira," she said, turning and flashing me a huge saccharine grin.

"See you later, Daphne," I said coolly.

She paused for a second and then walked out the door. Now that I knew it wasn't a done deal with Daphne working for Genevieve, I wanted that internship more than ever.

Chapter Five

I once asked my grandfather how he went from being thousands of dollars in debt after college to later running his own company (not at the Hughes level, mind you; he owned a chain of shoe stores). He told me it was all about having the right work ethic. While most zombies punch in and out, wish away the day, and live for the weekends, he threw himself into work wholeheartedly each and every workday.

"Be the first one there and the last one to leave," he advised when I called him the night before my departure. "Don't wait for someone to come to you—be proactive and seek out the work. Only then will people know they can count on you, and then you become indispensable."

As resident Xerox whore and gopher girl, I found it hard to imagine any intern becoming that irreplaceable. But when Gabe and Teagan popped by CeCe's office at the stroke of 4:59 P.M. to bail, I said I had more to do and that I'd meet them back at the ranch. They, along with all the other interns, were out the door so quick you'd think the building had a four-alarm fire—especially the Trumpettes, who vociferously announced their nightly plans upon departure: choice restaurant rezzies, nightclub lists, driver pick-up locations. They all went back to their various Upper East Side perches for disco naps before the preening process began.

But what would I be running off to, exactly? My depressing apartment? Another dinner I couldn't afford? That was a waste of time, because what I really needed to do was to show everyone at the magazine how committed I was so that I could get the internship. I was sure that CeCe would not give me glowing props to Genevieve—especially if Daphne was my competition. I had to meet some of the editors and network. It sounds kinda kiss-assy, but, frankly, none of the other interns cared that much.

First I wandered down by the accessories department. Richard was gabbing on the phone and I didn't want to interrupt him. Next I strolled to fashion, where I saw two editors on their knees packing for a Military Chic shoot.

"Hi," I started, suddenly getting a little nervous as the two girls, both so stylishly accessorized with layers of delicate chains and chunky belts, turned around. "I'm Kira. I'm an intern in the bookings department, with CeCe, and, um, I was wondering if you guys need any help?"

"No, I don't think so . . ." one said, wiping her brow while looking me over.

"Thank you so much, anyway," said the other, which I assumed was my cue to leave.

"Okay, thought I'd check just in case!" I said, turning around.

"Wait—" said the first one. "Actually . . . come to think of it, we still haven't unpacked the trunk from our Palm Bitch Acid Preppy shoot. Do you mind getting a start on that?"

"Sure!" I offered, beaming and psyched to be of use.

"There's no way you can finish tonight. I mean, there are piles and piles of things to be labeled, packed in bubbleopes, and returned to the fashion houses, but you might as well crack it open and get started."

The duo introduced themselves as Trixie and Lilly (Trixie was a petite Korean beauty and Lilly had almond eyes and chic shaggy brown hair). They were both in their twenties and were market editors at the assistant and associate level—probably what I would be right out of school, so it would be interesting to glean what they were typically up to.

I began the unpacking process, which was robotic but actually interesting. I opened velvet box after velvet box to find different pieces—pink and green bikinis, gold aviator sunglasses, sixties-era

Jackie O head scarves, and wedgie ribbon-tie espadrilles. Each piece had a corresponding Polaroid in the Palm Bitch shoot box, which catalogued all the pieces that were pulled, sent, and shot for the story. It yielded a four-page spread but involved weeks of work and tens of thousands of dollars in expenses: airfare to Florida, an alligator trainer for the Everglades shoot, a photographer with his assistant, hair and makeup artists, the model, and the stylists and their assistants.

As I checked off each piece, wrapped it, and filled out labels for the returns to the Michael Kors, Gucci, and Ralph Lauren public relations departments, I got a good rhythm going. And ninety minutes later, I was finished.

"So I'm done, I guess. Anything else?"

Trixie and Lilly turned around, stunned.

"Finished? *No way*," Trixie said skeptically, rising to survey my work. She must have thought I'd royally screwed up to have completed my task so quickly, but as she went over my packets and files, her eyes widened. "Lil, she just did this *all*," she said, jaw-on-floor. "Kira, you rock!"

Lilly got up and came over, too. "Oh my God. You are like Supergirl! You just saved us hours of work, you little Speedy Gonzales!"

I beamed. It wasn't rocket science—and it had been fun to see the inner workings of a shoot-in-a-box.

"And it's like seven o'clock! You are the best intern ever; you're working overtime for free," she added.

"Well, I have no life," I admitted. "I'm in New York for *Skirt*, so I might as well be at *Skirt*," I shrugged, hoping I didn't sound like the biggest dork on planet earth.

"Who else around here has no life?" a voice asked in the doorway. It was James, carrying a portfolio. "I feel like I'm in lockdown in Attica today. I haven't left my desk once."

"Hi, Jamesie," Trixie said. "Do you know Kira? This chick just cleared out this mammoth steamer in like under two hours. We worship her!"

"Yes, I know Kira," he said, giving me a trademark weak-in-the-knees-rendering smile. "And boy do I wish we had some help like that in the photo department. Our intern left at three o'clock. On a shoot day," he said.

"Oh, how's that Pier Sixty nautical chic thing going?" Lilly inquired.

"Fine, except the photographer's assistant just called to say they need more berets. Apparently some ship with sailors just pulled in and they want to use them with the models. I don't know where the hell to get berets. I hoped maybe you guys had some beret connection?"

"Not unless there's a huge logo on them. I mean, we have a few in the hat room from fall and winter," Trixie said. "But they're kind of for women. Not sailory at all—"

"The props warehouse is closed," said Lilly, looking at her watch. James looked defeated.

"What about that place Weiss & Mahoney?" I ventured. "I

read about it in *Time Out New York* once. Army surplus? I think they're open late. I can call."

"Didn't I tell you? This gal rocks," said Trixie.

I called the store and it was indeed open until eight o'clock.

"Great, that is so excellent. Thank you, Kira," he said, relieved. "Gotta run, good night, guys." He took off down the hall. Then I heard him stop and turn around, returning to our clothes-covered haven. "Hey, Kira?"

I turned from my piles of files.

"Ever been to a feature photo shoot before?"

Chapter Six

*O*kay, I have a newfound respect for models. I used to dismiss them as genetic mutants who were born blessed with killer bodies and perfect faces, and that was all they needed to get any guy they wanted and to secure enormous amounts of money. But believe it or not, there is work involved. Okay, don't cry them a river; it's not as tough as canning anchovies on an assembly line or mining for coal thousands of feet underground, but the catwalk is no cakewalk. Besides the actual standing around wearing skimpy clothing in freezing temperatures, people tell you that you look like crap all day. My self-esteem couldn't take it.

James and I arrived at the *Intrepid*, that ginormous ship that's famous for some reason or another, and we found the ten-thousand-dollars-a-day girls in bikinis contorting into unnatural poses. Some of the sailors were in the pictures, so they had their hands on the girls' butts or were holding some girls in their arms. Ick, it all seemed so uncomfortable. I'm sure the pictures will turn out amazing, but the idea that you'd be dangled over the Hudson River by some pervy sailor who hadn't seen a girl in ten months because he was out at sea and you're all oiled up in this embarrassingly teeny bathing suit—yuck! You couldn't pay me. Even ten grand. Okay, maybe for that fee I'd consider it. Not that anyone would pay ten *dollars* to see me in a bikini.

That aside, it was incredible to see all the action go down. For years I'd flipped through the pages of *Skirt* and been amazed by their magical photos, which were more creative and original than any other magazine. And to actually be there and watch the assistants running up and down, tucking in a collar, or tying a string on a bikini, or brushing aside an errant hair, was so interesting. I was psyched to see that the photographer was Jenny Toushé (pronounced *Touchay*), whose pictures I had always admired.

On the cab ride down to the army surplus store, James and I really didn't have a chance to chat much because his cell phone was ringing off the hook, first with photographers, then with editors, and so on. I was waiting for the moment when Daphne would call, but she didn't, and I was glad. It wasn't until we had successfully distributed the berets to the sailors and helped the fashion assistant pick up the entire rack of flippers that she had knocked over that James and I were able to sit back, watch the action, and talk.

"Thank you so much for bringing me to the shoot. It's amazing," I gushed as I watched Jenny snap away at a model with a snorkel in her mouth, walking the plank.

"No prob. Glad you could come. Thank *you* for saving my ass with the army surplus lightbulb."

"I could just sit here all night," I said, sighing and taking a sip of the coffee that James had so nicely brought me from the craft service table—a gigantic spread with a delicious catered buffet that, natch, no one but us had touched.

"Really?" asked James. "You don't find it boring?"

"Boring? Are you crazy? This is like a dream come true."

James looked at me and smiled. God, he was cute. The more I looked at him, how he was clad in the most well cut black pants I had ever seen and a Radiohead T-shirt, the more I resented Daphne and her ability to lay claim to everything I wanted.

"I love photo shoots also," he said. "Oddly enough, though, a lot of people find them boring."

I wanted to say "You mean Daphne?" but I had to bite my tongue. I wondered how he and Daphne had connected. What would she see in a photo assistant? Wasn't that beneath her?

"So how did you end up at *Skirt*?" I asked, feeling bold. He hesitated.

"Um, let's see . . . well, I've worked a lot on photo shoots . . ."

I nodded, and then he looked at me closely and leaned in.

"Okay, full disclosure. My stepfather's a photographer, he's done stuff for Hughes, and I got a lot of experience working for him."

"Aha!" I said with a sly smile. "So you're like a Trumpette?"

"Me? A Trumpette?" he asked with mock horror. I think he was about to defend himself and then changed his mind. "God, I guess so. Gross, I never thought of that."

"Denial," I said mischievously.

"Okay, okay, but let me defend myself."

"Go ahead," I said. God, I couldn't believe I was being so flirty with this guy. It was so not me.

"Yes, I got experience through connections, but I have worked my share of photo shoots, and I did toil away every summer during college paying my dues as a lowly assistant," he said, hand to heart.

"What, you worked for your stepfather?" I asked with a smile.

"Not only him," he said with a smile. "Avedon, before he died. Scavullo, Mario Testino. And then Wayne Priddy, this up-and-coming guy who rocks."

"Wow, you're lucky," I said. "That sounds amazing."

"But I also worked for Frank DeLine. You can't tell me that was a walk in the park. The guy only likes taking pictures of young gay guys, not to mention that he sexually harasses every guy who works for him. That was torture!"

"Okay, but who's your stepfather?"

"Victor Ledkovsky," he said almost meekly.

Victor Ledkovsky? He was, like, *the* photographer of all time. He did everything for Hughes Publications. I had torn his photos from magazines hundreds of times, worshipping his elegant pix of Natalie Portman on a horse, or his hilarious shot of Maya Rudolph getting doused with orange soda. The guy was talented and prolific; he made Annie Leibovitz look like a lazy amateur. The fact that James was related to him was a whole new ball game.

"I don't know what to say," I said, *really* not knowing what to say. God, now it all made sense. James was one of *them*. No wonder he and Daphne were together. They'd probably known each other since they were fashion fetuses.

"Come on!" he said. "It's not like that."

I think he could see that my expression changed. To hear that James was one of them, it almost made me think he was a little lame.

"Don't be unfair," James said, reading my mind. "I want you to know that even though I knew Mortimer Hughes and Genevieve West, I applied for my job at *Skirt* without any help from them. I have a different last name than Victor, and I didn't call Mortimer or use strings. I just sent in my application to human resources."

"Well, you seem to know what you're doing, so they obviously could sense a winner," I said, shrugging, giving him the benefit of the doubt. "And how did you meet Daphne? By a catwalk in Dior swaddling clothes or something?" I teased.

He laughed. "I knew her when we were young—not quite the diaper years, but in grade school tangentially—and then I went to boarding school in Europe. I met up with her again only when she came to visit the offices in December, when I started working here."

"Mm-hmm." I nodded.

"Kira, I know sometimes people think stuff when someone's going out with the boss's daughter. It's not like that. She's great and we have fun together. I just hope the rest of the office doesn't think that's how I hold on to my job. I'll probably end up having to work twice as hard to move up the ranks as it is," he confessed.

So Daphne was "great." Knife to my heart. No one wants any guy to tell them how crazy he is about another woman.

"You know," he said, flashing his huge grin. "I don't say these things lightly, but I have a feeling that you're going to do really well in this biz."

"Really?" I asked, instantly feeling my cheeks flush to a shade not unlike a strawberry.

"You're someone who's obviously got her stuff together and you have the confidence and taste to succeed. Not to mention that everyone is loving you," he said, standing up.

I looked up at him. Loving me? Everyone? Taste?

"More coffee?" he asked, holding out his hand. I handed over my cup.

"Thanks," I said.

I dreamily watched him walk over to the food table. God, he was cute. And he said I would do really well. And I really felt like he wasn't giving me a line, that he appreciated my style and me. And hell, it made me want him so badly. Why was Daphne Hughes the luckiest girl in the world?

Chapter Seven

I came home, starry-eyed but exhausted. I hiked up the stairs, thrilled to get to the top, as if I'd just scaled Everest, only to find a note affixed to our paint-chipped door: "Yo, Kira! We're around the corner at Milk & Honey—you better meet us there, beeyotch! XO G 'n' T."

I smiled and stood there on our doorway perch for a second. On the one hand, I felt so tired I was convinced I'd be comatose within seconds of hitting my prison cot. But on the flipside, I was in New York! I was young! I had the coolest job on earth! I could sleep when I was dead.

Milk & Honey, an unmarked speakeasy, was virtually impossible to find. I paced the whole block, peering down several rat-infested alleyways, before two giggling lovebirds emerged from a doorway. I watched them mack against a graffiti-covered wall as I squeezed by them into the hidden, crowded narrow bar. A DJ spun old-school eighties music as a cool crowd got down to the tunes. As I busted through to the back, I saw Teagan sipping a concoction and Gabe, naturally, dancing on his chair, voguing better than half of Madonna's dancers.

"*Yaaaaay!!* You made it!" he screamed ecstatically over the music, as if I were Angelina Jolie bringing foodstuffs to Sudan. "Girl, you get your butt up here and shimmy with me *this instant!*"

I looked at him, knowing there was no way I could muster up the energy to shimmy.

Teagan saw my face and laughed, offering me a seat next to her.

"Where have you been?" she asked.

"Well, I—" Just thinking of James, I was suddenly the purple rose of Cairo. "James took me to a shoot. It was so amazing . . ."

It took Gabe exactly 1.3 nanoseconds to jump down and sit next to me. "*Girl!* Oooooh, you got it *bad.* Look at her, Teags!"

Teagan nodded, her plum-painted lips curled into a sly smile. They so had my number.

"Guys," I said, shaking my head. "It's *sooo* not happening.

His dad is Victor Ledkovsky!"

"Shutterbug numero uno," Gabe marveled.

"Yeah, so that makes James fashion royalty." I sighed. "Just the perfect match for Princess Daphne."

"She blows," said Teagan with arms crossed. "She took three editors out for lunch today to Osteria del Circo! I mean, hellooo, buying the good recommendations for her Genevieve internship at all?"

"Total white-truffle-risotto-as-bribery," agreed Gabe.

"Well, there's nothing I can do but stay focused and plug along," I said. "That's what I came here to do—slave away, not chase some office crush."

"Yeah, but don't get your hopes up," said Teagan, before turning her back to Gabe and changing the topic to a dissection of some band.

Teagan's words stung. I liked her and Gabe, but it rubbed me the wrong way that they had already cast themselves as sort of renegade outsiders and made no attempt to ingratiate themselves to the Trumpettes or any of the editors who favored the Trumpettes. It's like they had chips on their shoulders. I didn't want Gabe and Teagan to classify me as one of them. It was too early to make allegiances. My sole focus right now was to get that internship.

And slave away I did. The next day I was sent to pick up CeCe's dry cleaning. Not from the dry cleaner. From the JFK Airport customs warehouse—she shipped her clothes to Paris because they had "the best dry cleaners on planet earth," according to her. Sheesh, talk about clothes being the love of one's life. I had never been to Paris, but all of CeCe's jackets had.

I was doing other various menial tasks throughout the morning when I heard Alida on an intern patrol. Sometimes, when a crisis would arise, Alida or some editor would yell, "Does anyone have a spare intern?" All the other interns suddenly made themselves scarce, pretended to be busy, or just plain hid in the bathroom. But not me. That morning I'd just finished calling twenty-three agency bookers to confirm go-see appointments for their models and was free to heed Alida's call.

"Hi, thanks, Kira," she said, frantic. "There is an emergency." She was breathless. "Liv Tyler's makeup artist's assistant's dog walker got sick with food poisoning from sushi and is foaming at the mouth!"

"Oh my gosh, what should I do?" I asked.

"I need you to go to the Carlyle, pick up the dog, and walk it before they get in the limo for the shoot."

I subwayed uptown in the scorching heat, got the pooch who was in the lobby with the second assistant waiting for me, and we strolled through the burning, sweat-inducing humid haze as I stopped every few steps to pick up the pellets of poo. Glamorous!

Back at the office, CeCe demanded I go buy her three pairs of panty hose. I know interns are the lowest level of scum at a fashion magazine, but I still resented the way she asked me—sorry, *ordered* me. At least have the common decency to say please. I trudged to Bergdorf, almost being mowed down by fanny-pack-wearing tourists, and finally returned with the goods and was about to collapse.

CeCe carefully examined the wares, nostrils aflare. "No! No! No!" she cried as if I'd just cut up her family pictures. "*Nooo!* I asked for Donna Karan *Collection*, not DKNY! This is the bridge line! You *idiot*! I have to do everything myself!" she scoffed before storming out into the hallway.

Standing by in head-to-toe Roberto Cavalli and Valentino, respectively, were none other than Daphne and Jane, who bore witness to the dramatic exodus. While Jane took a phone call on her rhinestone-studded cell, Daphne lingered by the doorway as I tried to retrieve the hose that CeCe had flung around the hall in her rage, raising her eyebrows in a condescending manner. "Don't worry," she said patronizingly. "You didn't know about bridge lines; it's okay. That means it's the designer's lower-priced, B-level line," she said.

"Yeah, I kind of knew that. I just didn't see anything but DKNY," I said in my defense. "She didn't really specify . . ."

"Here at *Skirt*," Daphne said as if she were ruler of the universe (though, stupid me, I guess she was), "just assume that editors don't need to specify. They *always* want the best." She smiled and nodded, happy to toss me the precious kernels of her wisdom, and sauntered off. I saw James had turned the corner and had seen the scene, so I turned on my nondesigner heels and retreated to CeCe's office.

Still fuming over first CeCe's and then Daphne's attitudes, I sought out something to keep my mind busy. I soon found Alida, who was on her hands and knees going through files. I took over, alphabetizing them perfectly so she could go get a blow-out before meeting her boyfriend. Before I knew it, it was eight o'clock. I was about to leave when I saw a light on in Richard's office.

"Hi, sweets!" he said, surprised to see me. "Where's your posse?"

"Oh, they left. Everyone's gone, I just thought I'd check if you need anything."

"No, no, it's okay," he said. "I have to take Polaroids of all these new accessories and I'm wiped out working on my new story."

"I can take them," I offered, content to distract myself from the embarrassing debacle by plunging into work mode. Before Richard could object, I sat down to organize the piles of bags, hats, scarves, gloves, and wallets for fall. I snapped away and catalogued the goods for an hour as he worked at his desk on jewelry layouts for a big bling story.

The entire time, I was brooding over the mishap with CeCe's stockings and how irate I was that Daphne had witnessed the whole scene. I knew that Daphne would always have an easy life, getting everything she wanted without ever trying, but I prayed that this internship wasn't part of it. There had to be some karma somewhere out there, right?

After a while, we heard footsteps coming down the hall.

"That you, whore?" Richard asked.

James appeared in the doorframe. "Oh, am I whore now, Richard?"

"Ooops, sorry, James. Thought you were that skank Fifi. Why're you here?"

"I went out for a bit but had to pop back to finish up, and was about to head home when I saw your light," James replied as he caught sight of me on the floor. "What are you still doing here?" he asked. "I think you just may be the most devoted intern in the building, Miss Kira." Why did hearing my name come from his mouth give me chills?

"Just helping Richard."

"You're a lucky man," James said to Richard. "Kira is the best. They just don't make 'em like you. I wish my intern stuck around past four o'clock! Well, bye, guys," he said, and left to go as he caught my eye. "Have a good night, Kira."

Two beats later, Richard launched. "Can you believe that hottie is banging that little brat?" he said. "Gagsville."

I smiled, not wanting to tip my hand about my would-be swoonfest over James, but nodded knowingly and kept working.

"Genevieve's been in Paris and I just know when she gets back she'll give that Daphne whatever post she wants," he said. "What a brat."

"You really think Daphne will get the internship?" I asked.

Richard smiled at me sympathetically. "You want it?"

"It's, like, my dream job," I confessed.

"I will totally put in a good word for you, sweets. I hate to be a heartbreaker, but you should know that Daphne really rules the roost here. It's lame, but true."

"So you think it's not even worth trying?" I asked, dreading his answer.

"You should totally try. You never know," said Richard encouragingly. But I had a sinking feeling that he *did* know.

48

Chapter Eight

"*Y*ou're quite the little worker bee, aren't you?" asked Daphne. Her tone was friendly, but I sensed a more sinister undercurrent.

"I don't know, that's what we're here for, right?" I asked.

We were in the conference room, organizing samples from ten young and up-and-coming jewelry designers whom Alida wanted Genevieve to feature in the magazine. I had been typing up call sheets for the following week's Zebra Power shoot when Alida popped her head in CeCe's office to borrow me. I was so psyched when she explained the mission, and congratulated myself on all my extra hard work that I was sure prompted me to be chosen. But all happy feelings deflated when I saw that Daphne was also assigned to the task. We'd been working together for an hour, lining up pendants, necklaces, and bracelets, mostly chitchatting about the fact that Jessica Simpson had been chosen for the next cover. We both agreed that it was a bad move on Genevieve's part. Jessica was *so* not *Skirt*. Everything was actually going well until Daphne decided she was done and plopped down on the couch.

"I like your attitude," said Daphne. Her tone was definitely that of a boss talking down to an employee.

"Thanks," I said.

As I lined up some jade earrings, I noticed Daphne playing with her Elsa Peretti heart pendant and eyeing me before glancing down at her watch.

"You know what, Kira?" she asked with grave importance. "I want you to come to lunch with me and my girls today."

She announced this in such a way that she sounded as if she had just given her kidney to someone on dialysis. But regardless, I was kind of flattered. It was weird, because I knew in my heart of hearts that Daphne was a totally self-serving manipulative person, but I was intrigued to find out if there was more to her than that. Okay, I know it seems like that thing when the popular girl suddenly notices you and all reason goes out the window. But the popular girl is popular for a *reason*. Sure, Daphne's father owned the place, but was that really all there was to her? I'm sure Cecilia's and Jane's parents were something major also, and yet they were like children of the corn, blindly following Daphne around. And what about James? There must be something he saw in her to date her. He hardly seemed superficial. Plus, I couldn't help but wonder why she was suddenly interested in *me*. This was my chance to figure her out.

"Um, okay, that sounds good," I said, finally. I could only imagine what Gabe and Teagan would say.

"I'm very excited. This, I think, will be fun," she said, giving me an appraising look as she stood up.

"Great," I responded tepidly, and with that, Daphne tossed her Chanel bag over her shoulder and we headed to the restaurant.

My heart sank when I glanced at the prices on the menu. Thirty bucks for pasta? That was so decadent. I was kind of regretting this lunch. I barely liked the company, and to have to dole out that much cash? Daphne must have noticed my face because just as I was scanning for a salad and realizing the cheapest thing on the menu was a side order of boiled spinach, she leaned in and said:

"And lunch is on me, my treat."

"No, it's okay," I protested.

She waved her hand in the air. "No, no. I took you to a really nice place, and I insist on paying. So order what you want."

"Thanks," I said softly. Phew.

"So Kira, we hardly know you! Tell us about yourself," said

Daphne, focusing her attention on me after we placed our order.

I looked across the table at Jane and Cecilia, who were nodding with serious faces, urging me on with the same intensity that Dr. Phil uses to urge child molesters to fess up.

"Well, um, what do you want to know?" I asked.

"Do you have a boyfriend?" asked Jane.

"Not right now," I said. I didn't really want to get into *that* topic.

"Any love interest?" Daphne asked, her eyebrow arched. Yes, I wanted to say, I want *your* boyfriend.

"Not really. I'm kind of, you know, burying my head in right now, trying to work. But what about you guys?" I asked, turning my attention to Jane and Cecilia.

They were much more eager to talk about themselves (enough about me) and launched into a diatribe that lasted through our entrees. Cecilia was deciding between two guys, both really gorgeous and with private jets, she pointed out. Vasilis was a Greek shipping heir who once dated Brittany Murphy (she told me that three times, as if that gave him street cred) and he *adored* her, but she wasn't sure if he could be faithful. Then there was Max, who was so fun and owned a really cool club downtown, but he didn't have a country house, and what was she supposed to do on the weekends? Her parents had been incredibly foolish and bought their estate in the rolling hills of central Connecticut, which, although trendy now and worth millions more than they paid for it (she assured me), was super boring. She wanted to be by the beach.

Jane had been dating Percy Fairbanks, a British lord (second cousin to Prince William) for two years. He was the *sweetest* guy in the world but her parents couldn't stand him because he hadn't gone to college and had no future plans. He was thirteenth in line for the throne, so he'd have to off the twelve dudes in front to even get a crown. Her parents wondered what she would have to talk about with him in the years to come. Judging by how dim Jane seemed, I couldn't imagine it would be a problem.

Then Daphne took her turn. "Well, you know I'm going out with James. He's Victor Ledkovsky's stepson, which is so funny that we have the whole fashion thing in common."

Right. Hilaaarious!

"But James's real dad is Matthew Carlson—you know, *the* Matthew Carlson."

Of course I knew who *the* Matthew Carlson was. He founded Carlson Airlines and Carlson Movie Theaters. That was James's father? God, I never would have guessed. This was even more strange than the stepfather connection. He was so low-key, whereas his father was a total publicity whore.

"They're not close, but he's, like, his only son, so he's still his heir," said Daphne, nodding her head as if Matthew Carlson might have some little bastard baby somewhere who was polishing a gold pacifier, readying for a fight for Daddy's dough.

"Right," I said. "So what is it you like about James?"

"He's really sweet. Very caring, very thoughtful," she stated, almost as though she were reciting the facts.

"He's such a doll! He gets her little gifts all the time," squealed Jane.

"And those letters he writes you!" added Cecilia. "I would die if one of my men wrote those."

Daphne nodded, pleased. "Yes, sweet."

I nodded along with them, burning with jealousy. It struck me that Daphne wasn't swooning or giddy about James at all; it was more cold, like he was some trophy boyfriend thanks to his DNA, not his charms.

"You know what, Keerster?" asked Daphne. "We need to set you up. Girls, who do we have for Kira? She's so chic and pretty, we gotta find someone good."

I suddenly felt flattered. Daphne thought I was chic and pretty? All along I had thought she considered me lame and beneath her.

"What about Michael Martone?" asked Jane.

"Michael Martone . . ." repeated Daphne, considering the suggestion with squinted eyes and a slow nod, as if imitating Rodin's "The Thinker." "That could be good. He's cute, and his dad owns one of the big studios. Paramount? Universal? I forget. That's a good idea."

Despite myself, I suddenly had images of me and this Michael Martone, hand in hand, walking into a premiere in Hollywood as the crowds parted for the son of the studio chief.

"Leo's single again," said Jane, eyebrows raised.

Leo? As in DiCaprio?

"Oooh, good one," said Daphne.

Oh my God, already I felt like my fortune was changing. What if I started dating a movie star? That would be too cool. Okay, my mind was racing. But I realized that it felt nice hanging out with Daphne, Jane, and Cecilia. If I was friends with them, I would have a whole different summer experience. Granted, they were self-involved and, for rich people, surprisingly obsessed with other rich people, but they were actually pretty nice. And even their vapid comments were more amusing and harmless than vicious. They called me pretty and wanted to set me up with Leonardo DiCaprio! That wasn't so bad. I had to be on my guard, of course, but what if I had been wrong about them? Maybe I was too judgmental. Maybe I was just jealous so I was being extra-critical. I mean, what could they be using *me* for? To get a good deal on a house in suburban Philly from my mom? Doubt that. It hardly made sense that Daphne would butter me up for something. Maybe she sensed I was competition for the intern in the editor in chief's office, but I doubt that she'd go to extremes to befriend me. Besides, I didn't want to overanalyze everything like I normally do. Sometimes, you just gotta say carpe diem.

"Okay, that's our summer mission, gals," said Daphne. "Kira, you're not going to slave away at the office anymore. I refuse to let you work late. You're coming out on the town with us, and you're going to get yourself a hottie!"

I admit, I was tempted. Not that I wanted to sell my soul for a guy, but why *not* go for a hottie?

"Yes, and you'll have much more fun with us than those weird Cotton nerds you have to live with," said Cecilia. I suddenly felt very uncomfortable.

"I know, that guy Gary?" asked Jane.

"Gabe," I said quietly. Immediately I felt my enthusiasm diminish. I did not want to engage in a bash-fest.

"Yeah, him. He has that total hick thing going on, like he's popped out of the Midwest and decided he's gay and is just going for the total faggy thing. It's so over-the-top," said Jane. Poor Gabe. I realized in that moment, although I hadn't known him long, that I really liked him.

"I know. Reign it in," said Daphne.

"He's a really good guy," I said firmly.

Daphne looked at me curiously, and I could sense that she was surprised I stood up for him. Finally she spoke. "Maybe we just don't know him."

"And what's up with angry Goth girl?" asked Cecilia. "It's like she's seen too many movies. Give it up." Now they were skewering Teagan. I looked down at my lap and shifted in my seat, wanting to press the "eject" button.

"Whatever," said Daphne, again waving her hand in the air. I could tell she liked to do that when she didn't want to hear any conversation that annoyed her. She turned to me. "You don't have to worry about them. I mean, of course you can be friends with whomever you want, but hang with us if you want to have fun and see the real New York. We're your new posse now."

I wasn't happy that they were so harsh on my roommates because I knew deep down that Gabe and Teagan were much more genuine people than my lunchmates. Then again, Gabe and Teagan weren't exactly going easy on the Trumpettes, either. It wasn't a crime if I hung out with them every now and then. So they're not the brightest bulbs on the porch. So maybe some ulterior motive will pop up and I'll realize why they singled me out. Until then, why not have some fun?

Chapter Nine

*T*he next night, Daphne 'n' company brought me to what they promised would be "the most amazing party ever" at their friend's parents' apartment. It was a stunning duplex on the Upper East Side, and although the décor was not exactly my style (I'm not into all that American folk art stuff, but I do appreciate it as an art form), the scale and views were breathtaking. I had been promised that there would be "a ton of hot guys there," but there were only about four totally wasted frat-boy types—who were more interested in taking bong hits than talking—and about ten nervous, completely decked-out girls who were vying for their attention. I bailed pretty quickly.

It was weird that Daphne never seemed to hang out with James. But Daphne said he wasn't crazy about her friends, and I could see why. So far they'd proven to be superficial and kind of vacant. I still had my doubts about Daphne, but of late she had been nothing except nice to me. Gabe and Teagan were totally giving me crap about hanging with "the Enemy." They accused me of trying to suck up to the boss's daughter—even though I explained that I just wanted to see how the other half lived, they'd give me an eye roll. It was hard, because it felt so high school to have to choose sides.

On Wednesday, I hit the town with Gabe and Teagan. We went to Williamsburg, the hipster capital, to a club called Lux, where the Scissor Sisters were playing. We Cotton interns all established early on that we worshipped them, so when they announced an impromptu tiny show, we jumped at the chance to snag tix. After work, I mentioned it to Daphne, who had invited me to go out clubbing with them at Marquee, but when I told them I was Brooklyn-bound she was in shock.

"Huh? Like seven-one-eight-land?" Daphne marveled of the non-Manhattan area code. "I sooo don't do outer boroughs," she said, laughing. "Be careful! Aren't there, like, bullets flying there?"

Anything outside the confines of Fifth Avenue was like *Deliverance* to her.

We got decked out in our glammest duds (including a newly

scored MAC glittery gray shadow for me pilfered from the beauty closet, my one job perk so far) and hit the L train. When we got to the club, the crowd was as sexy and cool as the people at *Skirt* but even edgier because instead of expensive designers, everyone wore an amalgam of vintage threads and duds from up-and-coming designers—like maybe their roommates. A lot of local bands had original costumes made by the other artists in their community, and the onstage look was finally getting exciting again. Like rock stars should be.

As the lights dimmed, the crowd roared, and the band took the stage, Gabe started screeching with glee. It truly was an amazing show. I loved how the music transported me, and I danced along. *This is what it's all about.* Here I was in New York, going to a concert, working at *Skirt*. Could life get any better? As the band played on, Teagan and I screamed and danced until I thought I would pass out. And just as I felt I couldn't be more into the night, I felt a tap on my shoulder.

"Kira? What are you doing here?"

It was James! He looked gorgeous. His black boots, dark blue painter's pants, and cool gray long-sleeve T-shirt with a Japanese rock band on the front made him look so kissable.

"I'm here with Gabe and Teagan," I said, grabbing them mid-dance and pulling them over to join me. "How 'bout you?"

"I knew Ana—the guitarist—back in San Francisco when I worked there."

All three of us screamed in unison: *"No way!"*

James laughed. "Way. Want to meet her after?"

Is the Pope Catholic? *Yes!*

Cut to us all backstage in the greenroom, jaws on the floor. We met the band and had the best time. They couldn't have been more gracious with the effusive compliment-fest that we bestowed upon them. But the best part was just hanging with James and watching him with his friends. He was way more relaxed than he was at work, which I suppose is understandable. It's not like he's uptight, but he is kind of businessy, which is how you should be.

Finally it was Cinderella pumpkin time for me. Naturally, Gabe (who literally had a Niagara Falls of drool talking to Jake, the lead singer) refused to depart at such a tender hour (one o'clock A.M.) and Teagan wanted to stay, too.

I told James that while this was the best night ever, I needed to go back and get some z's for another big day toiling away at *Skirt*.

"That's okay," he said. "I'm actually exhausted. Come on, I'll drive you back." Wheels? Score.

Gabe gave me a very unsubtle smirk as I left, and James held the door for me as we walked out. The mild summer air amplified by the East River's current blew over us.

"This breeze is such a nice relief from that sweaty club!" I gushed, pushing the hair out of my face.

"Yeah, it's pretty cool you guys could deal with that mosh pit," James said with a grin. "Daph would probably have freaked. I don't blame her, though. It gets tight for sure. You just have to sur-render to the crowd, I guess."

"I think she said she's at Marquee. Doesn't that place get crowded?" I asked.

"Not the way she does it. Table service, a bottle of Dom— it's pretty spacious at that level." He smiled. I noticed he wasn't reverent of the VIP booth but rather semiscoffing.

We got to his car—a Ford hybrid (he was green; so hot!)—and as we drove, I drank in the blinking lights of the majestic skyline in front of us.

"This is so beautiful," I said. "What a New York moment."

"Yeah, it's a bummer how many New Yorkers never get to see it, though," he said wistfully. "You know, they get kind of stuck in their patterns—never leave their little pod and just get out and breathe. Or get to see a view like this . . ."

We rode in silence for a second, and I couldn't help but won-der if that was a remark about Daphne.

"It's cool you're willing to explore, that you don't feel bound to one small zip code," he said, looking over at me.

"Well, I think some people from here take it for granted. I just want to gobble it all up. It sounds so cheese but I have dreamed about living here," I admitted.

"It's not cheese!" he said, looking at me, smiling. "It's great. People like you are the ones who keep New York fresh and edgy and exciting."

I didn't know how to respond, though I feared my pink cheeks were doing the talking.

"It's funny to me that you work at *Skirt*," I said, breaking the quiet.

"Really? Why?" he asked, glancing at me out of the corner of his eye as we crossed the bridge.

"Well, I know you're into photography, and it's, like, in your step-blood, but it seems like you have a lot of other interests."

"You're right. I do love photography, and obviously *Skirt* is a great magazine for that, despite the critics who disparage fashion magazines, but I don't know. It was just something that I had done; it came easily to me, I know a lot about it, and it was a job out of college. I don't really see working there as a career, though."

"So you want to branch out, do something totally different?" I asked, amazed at how comfortable I felt with him to be giving him the third degree.

"Maybe," he said, pausing for a second before blurting out, "I'd secretly love to be a musician." I swear, his face reddened. "Don't tell anyone," he added hastily.

"A musician? That's cool."

"I know, pipe dream, but that's how I got to be such good friends with Ana. We took guitar lessons from the same teacher in San Fran. But I don't think it will happen," he said, shrugging.

"Why not?" I asked, the image of him strumming a guitar burning in my mind.

"How many people are actually successful at that?" he said. "At least with photography I know I can make a living."

"You gotta follow your passion. I mean, hello, you're not like fifty with a mortgage and kids' tuitions. No better time than the present to try something that you've always wanted to do."

"I don't know," he said, clearly wanting to change the subject, so I dropped it.

I wonder if he had ever fessed up to Daphne about this. Probably. And most likely she shot him down. I would never if he was mine. How hot would it be to have your guy singing up on stage? Tingles.

We rode in silence for a little while until I directed him to my abode. I watched his arm guide the stick shift and almost melted. I couldn't help it—something about him, his warmth, his smile, his cute dorky envirocar, made me swoon.

"This is it," I said, pointing to the graffitied wall of my building. "Hovel sweet hovel."

He smiled. "Kira," he said, and I pictured the letters of my name melting as if made of chocolate, "you have a great way with words."

Goosebumps.

"I appreciate the lift," I said, getting out. "Sure beat the train. Thanks for keeping my evening rat free."

James's eyes widened suddenly as his face registered shock.

"Look out behind you! There's one!"

I shrieked, instantly picturing a pack of canine-size rodents devouring me alive. James started laughing.

"I'm kidding, Kira," he said, hopping out of the car. "I'm

sorry, I couldn't resist."

I made a fake-angry face and crossed my arms. "Jerk."

"Here, I'll walk you to the door and make it up to you."

We walked up to my crack house slash residence as I fumbled for my keys. "I promise to slay any rodents that cross your path, milady," he vowed.

"Thanks, Sir Lancelot," I said, looking at him bathed in the light of the street lantern. "Seriously. For everything. That was so much fun."

"The pleasure was mine," he said, turning back down the stairs. "Sweet dreams, Guinevere."

Chapter Ten

*B*ack at work, I felt like a double agent—bosom buds on the surface with Daphster and posse, but *really* pals with my Cotton Club gang. Gabe and Teagan eagerly awaited choice Trumpettes quotables, particularly from Cecilia, who was ripe with shockers ("Flying commercial is soooo D," "Bouley is my cafeteria!" and the even more insane "Gucci is my Gap").

I wasn't entirely sure why Daphne had decided to extend the olive branch of friendliness my way, but despite the chasm between her life and reality, at least she was entertaining. Her constant pronouncements ("Animal prints are only acceptable on accessories") seemed to be taken as gospel by all, sometimes even by me. But as I pretended to just be mellow buddy-buddy during a Daphne-organized fashion show of a new rack of fall samples, I kept my eye on the prize: the job at Genevieve's desk. Sure, I'd taken a bit longer lunch breaks a couple of times and even left at five once or twice, but I knew what I wanted and still did everything to get there. We'd be finding out the lucky winner in two days at the intern staff meeting, and I hoped I'd finally be saying au revoir to CeCe, the raging, demeaning beeyotch, and bonjour to the plum assignment. I just hoped Daphne wouldn't be weirded out that I'd landed the gig over her. She'd probably be pissed and boot me from her little power clique, but quite frankly, even the alluring charms of her lifestyle—while enticing—would not eclipse the reason I was there. Nor could my sweet crush on her boyfriend, which I'd decided to ignore for now.

Gabe, Teagan, and I got to head home early one night, released from our duties because of some major Hughes Publication staff party that everyone was invited to but the interns.

"So are you and the Trumpettes like friends now?" Teagan asked after I had just relayed the latest fashion pronouncement from Daphne.

"We're not friends, but we are," I said, confusing even myself with that statement.

"Then why do you rag on Daphne?" asked Teagan.

I sighed. I liked Teagan, but her tone could be challenging. I knew she didn't mean it, but she had a tendency to make people feel defensive.

"I don't know. I think some of the things she says are really outrageous, but they're harmless. She's like Jessica Simpson."

"I find her really shallow," said Teagan.

"I think she's smart," said Gabe. "She just doesn't know what to do with herself, since she's been given everything."

I felt bad that Gabe was defending Daphne, especially after she had been so harsh about him. I immediately wanted to change the topic.

"Any news on your college sitch?" I asked Gabe. I knew that he had talked to his parents for a long time the previous night, and I hoped he had told them about his change of plans.

"I wanted to, but I couldn't. I don't know what will freak them out more, my homosexuality or that I'm not going to school near them. I'm in denial."

"You'll be fine," I assured him as we made our way through the turnstile.

"Don't worry," said Teagan soothingly. "You're a great guy and your parents know that. You'll get through this." That was Teagan for you—just when she really annoyed me, she would then turn around and be a total sweetheart.

I was really lucky that these two were my roommates. Really lucky.

Chapter Eleven

*J*ane popped by CeCe's office as my boss was taking Polaroids of a sad-looking Estonian who was perched on the window-side stool like a scared crane.

"Just get a whole new mouth full of choppers and we'll see. You have potential," mused CeCe aloud as she handed me the girl's card for her wall of "maybes." "We just have to get a great color job 'cause your hair couldn't be more mousy. And you need a facial like an orchid needs water. Speaking of which, start drinking fifteen glasses a day now."

"Hi, CeCe!" said Jane from the doorway. "Can I steal Kira away for some eats?" Her voice was loaded with charm and she batted her eyelashes as if asking Daddy for the keys to the Rolls.

CeCe had been looking at me through a new lens lately. She could see that I had been slowly absorbed into Daphne Hughes's gang and therefore went easier on me than she usually did. "Sure! Take her," she said as if she were handing off a used Kleenex for disposal.

I followed Jane out to the elevator landing where Daphne and Cecilia were waiting.

"Hey, Keerster," Daphne said, looking me over. "I'm loving that kilt. It's all about tartan for this fall, you know," she pronounced. "Oh! And Jamesie said he saw you last weekend! So funny you guys were both like slumming it! Hilarious." But the way she said *hilarious* sounded like the news of our run-in was anything but.

"Guys, sorry, but I don't think I can go to lunch," I said. I was annoyed that Jane had dragged me out of CeCe's office. I mean, yes, CeCe sucked, but I had work to do, and while I did want to be friends with Daphne and co., I didn't want to be considered a "Trumpette." I was worried that all of this time away from the office could not look good.

Daphne's eyes narrowed. "What do you mean?"

"I just . . . I promised Richard I'd help him sort through the new Sergio Rossi shoes that just came in, and Alida asked me to help her with her Baby Heiress shoot."

Daphne's nostrils flared ever so slightly. "Alida asked you to help her on that?" Her voice was tight.

"Yeah," I said.

Daphne stopped and flipped her hair. "Interesting. Are you going to the shoot?"

"I don't know." What was going on?

"Is that the one Orlando Bloom will be at?" Jane asked Daphne.

"Yes," said Cecilia.

Daphne was studying me carefully in silence.

"Is there a problem?" I asked.

"Why would you think there's a problem?" asked Daphne, her voice sarcastic.

"Okay . . ."

"Look, if you don't want to go to lunch with us, just say you don't want to go to lunch with us," said Daphne.

I felt suddenly nervous, and I hated that. Why was Daphne all pissed off? Did *she* want to go on the shoot?

"It's not that. I just have work to do," I said.

"Kira, I *own* the magazine. If I want my friend to go to lunch with me, then there are no questions asked."

I didn't know what to say to that. She was acting so strange. Cecilia and Jane stared at me, unsure of what to do.

Just then, Alida walked by. Daphne turned to her with a grim smile.

"Alida, do you mind if Kira takes a lunch break?" she asked in a fake sweet voice.

"Um, no, of course," said Alida, giving me a strange look as she walked away.

"See?" said Daphne.

"Come," said Jane finally, but in a meek voice.

Cecilia nodded.

"Fine," I said.

"Great," said Daphne, walking ahead. "I want to go to Lever House."

I didn't want to go. And I felt torn the entire time we walked to the restaurant, knowing it was against my better judgment to do so. Jane and Cecilia seemed clueless, chattering on the entire time about some hot guy they had met at their beach club and wondering how much money he was worth. Daphne barely said a word, and I could only imagine what was going on in that mind of hers. I figured her out all right—she *was* just as manipulative as I'd originally suspected. Clearly the fact that I was being involved in such high-profile projects was a threat to her. And what was up with that comment about James? Was she jealous? It seemed strange to think it, but I now felt like I had confirmation that Daphne had befriended me so that I would not work as hard. And she was trying in her own little way to take me down.

When we got to the café (another fifty-bucks-a-head joint) they all ordered their usual piles of leaves.

"You guys know Madeline Cobb, right? She has *serious* ka-ching: G-5, manse in Montauk, thirty-room triplex on Fifth, sick house in Aspen, ski-in, ski-out," marveled Jane. "You know, her family invented the Cobb salad."

I was fed up with this inane chatter and finally spoke up.

"But it's not like they get royalties every time someone orders a Cobb salad," I thought aloud.

The three girls considered this fact and shrugged. It was kinda weird how someone with billions herself would sit and count other people's money. I guess the rich want to know their peers.

Daphne remained unusually quiet through the rest of the lunch, while Cecilia and Jane continued to gossip now about which heiress's dad was banging the secretary and who had a prenup. All the while I looked at my watch. As we got up to leave, my heart rate started to spike as I realized that I had just wasted a good hour and a half on this stupid lunch. A lunch with girls I was starting to intensely dislike.

Chapter Twelve

I avoided Daphne the rest of that tense afternoon. The next morning, I set up shop in the closet, sorting through scarves for Trixie, when I heard my name. I quickly darted into the refrigerated fur-vault section of the closet, ducking around a corner and behind a rack of boas and scarves, out of view but still within earshot.

"Kira's just so lame-o," declared Daphne. "I mean, I thought she was cool but then it's like, ditch the dorks and get with the picture, girl!"

"Totally," Jane concurred. I doubted she ever had thoughts of her own. If Daphne worshipped me, I was sure Jane would think I was the bomb, too.

"She's just so, like, ass-kissy. Have you noticed how she stays late? Like what does she think, she's gonna get a job here?" asked Cecilia.

"Whatever. She's from, like, Nowheresville, USA."

Now my blood was boiling. Philly, city of brotherly love, home of the Liberty Bell, the best cheesesteaks on earth, and Rocky Balboa, was *Nowheresville*? Uh, not exactly, hon. It's a booming metropolis! And plus, even if I had been from East Jesus, Texas, who cares? Most people in fashion didn't come from New York.

"Who are you guys talking about?" James entered, crunching on an apple. "You always seem to have a voodoo doll of the moment, you three."

"Ugh, James, don't be such a righteous good guy. It's no fun." Daphne pouted. "Plus, Kira is such a powerdork, she deserves it."

"Kira?" he asked, sounding surprised. How many voodoo dolls did Daphne have in her toy chest? I shuddered behind a giant sheared mink stole. "She is awesome. What's your problem with her?" James asked.

"Whatever," said Daphne. "She's so *not*. She's a little climber loser. Plus, I think she and her Goth friends are stealing from the closet. New stuff's been missing. I saw them in here yesterday. You do the math."

"Come on, Daphne," James said, incredulous. "It's one thing for you to shamelessly rag on her for no reason but another entirely for you to make up lies and accusations like that. That is totally unfair."

75

"What are you, standing up for her now?" Daphne sneered. I could almost picture her angry face, nostrils aflare. I bet people rarely challenged her.

"She's really cool, Daphne. She's not a thief."

"How the hell do you know?"

"I know. She's not the type to steal. She's one of the good guys," he said, almost quietly.

Daphne sounded incensed. "Well listen, James, you can take your *good feelings* and kiss off. I don't need this bullshit. I'll have you know I met Ralph Lauren's middle son's best friend at a party last night and he was dying to hook up with me."

"Well, that's great news," James said, almost laughing. "Happy polo playing." I heard him walk out, and then there was a pin-drop silence.

"Oh my God, total craziness," Jane said nervously.

"Whatever," Daphne said defensively. "His stepdad is, like, so over anyway. I mean he hasn't shot a cover for us in, like, *months*. C'mon, let's go hit Remi for lunch."

With that, the trio, including a seemingly unwounded Daphne, took off in their five-inchers. I still had chills from the emotional arrows shot through me but was healed at the thought of James's valiant protestations. It was all very Sir Galahad. What I had overheard, though, made it very clear that Daphne had it in for me after yesterday's lunch. I wasn't looking forward to being an enemy of the head Trumpette.

Chapter Thirteen

*I*t was time.

All of the interns were gathered around the conference room table over which Alida presided. Everyone sat nervously as other announcements were made. ("Please, guys, do not flush tampons!")

"And now, the moment some of you have been waiting for these past two weeks—"

The door opened and in walked the elusive Genevieve West. We had never seen her before; she was either at the couture collections in Paris or at shoots or Valentino's yacht or Karl's house in Biarritz, so seeing her in person for the first time was like having one of the characters in your favorite book come alive. She was smaller than I had imagined, but of course that was silly—everyone at *Skirt* was tiny, and she should be no different. But she was only like five foot two and had not one extra ounce of fat on her. She had the straightest black hair I had ever seen, which fell to her shoulders and was cut off in a perfect line, with bangs cut just above her smallish dark eyes. Her lips were painted very red, and it appeared as if a smudge wouldn't dare happen on her face. Her nose was a little pointy, and actually, truth be told, she looked kind of like a witch, but she was so stylishly dressed in a perfect Chanel suit with delicate Manolo Blahnik heels, accessorized with a delicate diamond bracelet and earrings, that you didn't really notice her individual features and instead focused on the entire package, which spelled out success and power.

"Hello" was all she said as she looked us over. As her eyes hit mine, I looked down, suddenly bashful. She seemed remote and cool but not as scary as some had made her out to be.

"So interns, Genevieve—" Alida said. "After consulting with all the editors about the work done in the last two weeks, we have decided upon a girl who has gone above and beyond the call of duty—"

At that moment, James walked in carrying materials that Alida needed to sign off on. He quietly stood off to the side.

" . . . she has an exemplary work ethic, style, and, most of all, she is not afraid to be proactive and seek work," Alida continued in a measured, sober meter as Genevieve, James, and the whole office looked on. "In other words, she aims to please and succeeds. And that is why our head intern this summer, chosen by our editor in chief, will be—"

I felt heat rise in my cheeks as palpitations rang through my chest cavity.

"Daphne Hughes!"

Chapter Fourteen

"It's okay," Gabe cooed, holding my hair back as I leaned over the chipped porcelain toilet in our bathroom. "Do you want some more water?"

He handed me a cup and I gulped down the remaining liquid.

"Here're more towels," said Teagan, entering the bathroom. "You okay?"

I sat up. "I just can't believe it," I said for probably the two-hundredth time that night.

"We know," said Gabe, rubbing my back.

After Alida had said Daphne's name, it was as if time stood still. All I knew is that Daphne and her gang squealed and ran up to Genevieve, and I sat there dumbstruck. As it was near the end of the day, Gabe and Teagan quickly ushered me out of the building before the heaving sobs could come and brought me straight to our apartment, where I proceeded to get drunker than I ever have been in my life, thanks to a bottle of tequila Gabe had managed to buy from a shady liquor store nearby. I am not a big drinker; I'm not even legal. My parents let me have a glass of wine every now and then, but tonight I didn't care. I just did shot after shot (which is disgusting, by the way). And now I was paying the price.

"I think she's done barfing," Gabe said to Teagan.

"Let's get her up," said Teagan.

The next thing I knew they each had an arm around me and were practically carrying me into my bed. Teagan had put towels along the floor and squeezed a trash can into the minuscule space between my bed and the wall. Gabe pulled the cover over me and even kissed me good night.

As I lay there, the room spinning, I couldn't stop thinking about the afternoon's turn of events. I wasn't like Veruca Salt from *Charlie and the Chocolate Factory*, but my parents had always said work hard and you will get your rewards. It had proven true. Until now. I worked hard and got into Columbia, my dream school. I worked hard and got to be editor in chief of the school newspaper. I worked hard on my essay and got the Cotton internship for *Skirt*. And I worked hard and *didn't* get the internship in

Genevieve's office. It would be one thing if I had had a real competitor. But Daphne totally got the job just because of who she is or, more importantly, who her father is.

Okay, okay, I know I was warned. Gabe and Teagan told me countless times that Daphne had it in the bag. But I was naive. My problem is that I have too much faith in rules and regulations, you know, a strong sense of justice. I believe in taking turns, I believe in democracy. But that's not what the world is like, and I really learned that the hard way today.

I still couldn't get over their flagrant nepotism. "Welcome to the world," Gabe and Teagan had both said. So I guess this was growing up—learning that if you bust your butt, it's all for naught. I was pretty discouraged. I was also embarrassed. I had told everyone that I wanted the job. James knew, Richard knew, Alida knew, and Daphne knew. And now they all knew that I had failed. It was mortifying.

Why the hell did Daphne even need the internship? She was guaranteed a job there anyway. She was probably just that type of girl who needed to always get that golden ticket. Veruca Salt. Why couldn't she realize she didn't need this position to get where she needed to be? She could have just stepped aside and let me get it. I knew that wasn't realistic, but I wasn't feeling rational. My confidence was totally shaken. I just wanted to quit. The more I thought about it, the more that seemed like the right decision. Tomorrow morning I was going to tell Alida and leave. Sorry to disappoint the people at Cotton, but this girl was going Wool.

* * *

"I'm really sorry about this," Alida said, her voice extremely serious.

I had planned to go marching dramatically into her office and hand her a resignation letter, but before I could, she grabbed me and pulled me into the Xerox room.

"I am, too," I said, preparing to make my speech. Gabe and Teagan had been pleading with me all morning to change my mind, telling me it would be the stupidest thing I would ever do, that I was just being stubborn and defensive, get over it and forget the whole thing, and start having some fun this summer. But I was planning on ignoring their advice.

"Kira, everyone here knows you deserved that internship. I shouldn't be telling you this, so please don't repeat it, but we all know why Daphne got it," she said, pushing her hair behind her ear. "It's ridiculous, but our hands were tied. Let's face it: Her dad's our boss, and what she wants, he wants. It was a huge, huge scandal a few summers back when her stepsister didn't get it. This time, there was nothing we could do."

"I'm sorry to hear that, but it doesn't make it better for me," I said, feeling brave. "I worked really hard and I feel like I was robbed. So I have no choice—" But before I could finish, Alida cut me off.

"I know, and everyone here loooves you. So what I want to say is that even though this sucks, please don't leave or do anything silly, because we all totally want to recommend you for a job as

83

soon as you graduate from college."

A job? I blinked a few times, just to see clearly. *They loved me?* Suddenly, my shoulders collapsed and I felt as if I could breathe. "Really? Wow, I don't know what to say."

"It's true. So please, just stay the course, and keep doing what you're doing. I'm sure you feel the world is so unfair—and it can be, as you've seen—but it's the last battle that counts, and in the long haul, hard work is rewarded."

"Thanks, Alida. Thanks so much."

I was psyched. Okay, so good can come out of bad. Things can happen in a different order. When I exited the Xerox room, Gabe and Teagan were lingering, pretending to fax something so that they could find out what went down. I waited for Alida to be out of earshot before whispering, "It's all cool."

"Yay! So you'll stay?" asked Gabe.

"Totally."

We group hugged, but when we split apart I spotted Daphne waltzing in with a cup of Starbucks.

"Hey!" she said with a wave, before turning left toward Genevieve's office.

Although Alida had quelled my desire to bolt, I still felt that tingle of rage inside me.

Chapter Fifteen

*B*ack slaving in CeCe-land, my newly empowered ego was just beginning to wither again (amid her cries of "You idiot! You *know* we don't use redheads for beauty stories!") when Richard entered in a frenzy and announced in high-dramatic fashion that he was dyyyying and needed me "desperately" due to an unforeseen "crisis of epic proportions."

There wasn't much to say to that, especially with Richard's flailing limbs and woe-is-me stressface, so CeCe ceded possession of me. I nervously gathered my things and followed Richard obediently around the corner to the elevator. As the doors closed, he launched into an explanation.

"I have to go to this stupid accessories shoot called the Forensic Files—Genevieve wanted all the models to be like dead people in chalk outlines. Raymond Meier's shooting, he's a genius. He'll make it great. We got Marilyn Manson's makeup artist to do it. It should be cool," Richard rambled a mile a minute.

Huh? "But what was the crisis?"

"Nothing! I just wanted some company. If I'm gonna sit on my ass for six hours, I want a buddy with me. Oh, but you do have one duty: I'm giving you strict instructions to keep my fat ass away from the catering table!"

I smiled, exhaling, feeling so lucky to have bonded with Richard. "Thank you so much," I said, hugging him.

"Hon, like those McDonald's people say, you deserve a break today," he said, patting my head sweetly. "And speaking of cows, don't you dare let that Daddy's girl get you down, 'k?"

"Okay."

We hopped in a cab to the glamorous Industria Superstudio, a series of skylit lofts where some of the most famous fashion campaigns and magazine editorials are shot. In the hallway were mobs of people—models all in peacock feathers, little kids on a children's clothing modeling audition, and Jessica Alba, with her entourage, getting ready for a *Cosmo* shoot.

In the *Skirt* studio, I watched intently as the models lay cadaver-like on the floor with the pedicurist attaching toe tags while hair stylists tended to their locks. It was darkly fascinating, and I was kind of obsessed watching everything unfold.

One of the photographer's assistants saw me standing by and asked if I'd "be a dear" and run to the nearby Tortilla Flats to score some chips for the gang. Apparently the catering table was way too fancy-pants, with lobster salad on endive, lemon sea bass, and frisée salad. I nodded and obediently headed out on my errand.

As I walked around the corner, the warm breeze from the Hudson hit me and I suddenly felt happy I decided to stay. What the hell would I have done in Philly, anyway? It was too late in the summer to get a job. Just then, I saw a massive limousine pull up to a small restaurant about halfway down the block. I wondered if some actress was going to get out. Or a rock star. But I couldn't believe it when I saw Alida. With an older man. He looked familiar to me, but I didn't quite recognize him. He was short but powerful looking, with a gray suit and leather briefcase.

She followed him to the café door. Wait, was she seeing this older guy behind her boyfriend's back? I saw her look both ways before entering, and luckily she didn't catch me staring from the opposite corner. It definitely seemed like she didn't want anyone to see her. A sugar daddy? Hmmm . . . I was curious. But I decided to keep it to myself, since I knew how gossip lit up the fashion live wire with wagging tongues and stealthy whispers. It was none of my business.

I turned to enter Tortilla Flats after my streetside spy-fest and heard my name. It was James. I hadn't seen him since the big announcement. And though I knew he was well aware of the politics involved, I somehow felt embarrassed that I hadn't won the gig.

"Hey you," he said, breathless. "I just got to the shoot and they told me where you'd gone. Listen, Kira—" he said, following me to the ordering counter. We stood face-to-face under the bedecked ceiling crammed with Mexican streamers, tinsel, and trinkets. "Sorry. About that internship—" he continued, shrugging, "I know how hard you've worked."

"I'm over it," I said, shrugging away his concern. Sure, I was a big liar and still bitter, but Alida's words continued to be a soothing balm on the wound of rejection.

"That's good," said James, not quite believing me. He hesitated a second before saying, "You know, I'd be furious if I were you."

"You would?"

"Of course. The whole situation sucks. So transparent. Really lame."

"Thanks. It's good to know I'm not the only one who thinks so."

We placed our orders and a smug smile crept across my face. Daphne may have gotten the internship, but she'd succeeded in making some enemies along the way and lost a boyfriend—all because of me.

"Ready?" James said, opening the door for me.

"Ready," I nodded. And I was. As always, just talking to James made me feel better.

Chapter Sixteen

"*H*ow about this? It would look awesome on you with your cute little butt," said Gabe, holding up a gold lamé micromini.

"Um, I don't think so," I said, and continued to plunder through the racks of clothes.

"These are so genius," said Teagan, pulling brown leather sandals with a cork heel out of the shoe bin and trying them on for size. "Perfect fit!"

It was five o'clock on Teagan's birthday, and in a few hours we were planning to rage and blow off some serious steam. We were in the fashion closet at *Skirt*, scanning through all the clothes that had already been photographed and trying to find cool outfits to wear to our first trip to Melt, a hot new club in the Meatpacking District. While technically it was against the rules to borrow from the closet, *everyone* did it, including all of the top editors and Genevieve herself. Very little fashion was ever returned to the clothing designers who lent them out for shoots, and usually at the end of the season, people were permitted to take what "swag" they wanted. (There was a hierarchy, of course—more senior editors got to go first, then associates, assistants, and what was left went to the interns.)

"Oh my God, I have to have these!" squealed Gabe, trying on some strappy sandals. "They are just too sweet to pass up."

"Come on, you can't wear those," I said.

"Why? Because I'm a guy? Why do the girls get all the good stuff?"

"Here's a cool leather bracelet—this is unisex. Check it out," I said, tossing it to him.

"Fits like a charm," said Gabe. "*J'adore* Dior."

"What are you doing?" a voice from the doorway demanded. We all turned around. It was Daphne.

"Oh, hey, Daph, we're just messing around, trying on some stuff," I said casually.

Daphne's mouth contorted into a frown and she crossed her arms sternly. "You know you're not supposed to be in here without any editors."

Gabe and Teagan glanced at each other with looks of disgust, then shrugged.

"Come on, Daph, you know everyone checks out the closet," I said.

"I certainly hope you weren't planning on borrowing anything. That's against the rules and I would have to report you," she said, staring at me coldly.

I couldn't believe her. She had no idea that I overheard her bashing me in the closet, and nothing had been said between us about the internship. I'd played it cool and let her glory in her new status, content in the knowledge that the people who mattered to me knew the real situation.

"What's the deal, Daphne? Is something wrong?" Treat bees with honey, treat bees with honey.

I watched her flex her calf muscles, which she often did when she was wearing really high heels, and then saw her eyes move from me to Gabe to Teagan.

"There's been some theft of late. Genevieve is *really* concerned, and she asked me to look into it. In fact, she put me in charge of finding out who it is, and I'm working with management now, trying to crack the case. I would *really* hate to find out that one of you had something to do with it."

Oh. My. God. What a raging beeyotch. She'd hinted at something like this that day I'd overheard her, when she and James split up. Was she really going to sink so low?

Teagan and Gabe were too astonished to speak, so I had to.

"Daphne, of course we have nothing to do with it. We're merely trying on clothes, like you and Jane and Cecilia do *all the time*," I said, kind of losing my cool. "So if it's a problem for you, since you've essentially been assigned to be hall monitor, we will leave."

Teagan and Gabe followed me out. We brushed past her and left her standing on the threshold, arms folded, expression sour.

When we got downstairs we all burst out laughing.

"She is evil!" said Teagan. "What a diva whip cracker!"

"Can you deal with how she said she had to 'crack the case'? Is she Hercule Poirot now?" I asked.

"She's a total clam!" pronounced Gabe. "Actually, she's a *quahog*."

"A *what?*" laughed Teagan between guffaws.

"A quahog is a giant North Atlantic clam. With Daphne Hughes's spoiled face on it."

We giggled, picturing the heiress as a bottom-feeding mollusk.

Later that night we all put Daphne out of our mind and went to Melt, which was amazing. I was so nervous about using my fake ID. My cousin Charlotte had given me her driver's license, and she looked a lot like me, but I wasn't sure it was going to work. Gabe told me I was being *ridiculous* and that Charlotte and I were as similar as the Olsen twins, but my heart was pounding as Teagan and I followed a confident Gabe past the crowds of "201's and 516's," as Daphne would say, referring to the New Jersey and Long Island area codes. As we approached the velvet ropes, my hand shook as I retrieved Char, my drink-pounding, 2-D alter ego.

"We work for *Skirt*," said Teagan. Trixie and Lilly, the market editors, had alerted us to the fact that it worked magic if we ever wanted to cut a line. Clubs liked to be associated with the hippest publications on the planet, which made sense. It also usually worked for getting reservations at new restaurants and tickets for premieres.

The humongous bald bouncer barely even looked at Teagan or me, stopping only to inspect Gabe's butt, then shrugging and letting him in.

The club was cool, not like one of those thumping techno music places where you can't see or hear anyone, but more like a 1940s swanky lounge. The walls were wood-paneled, and leather booths featured on each table cute little lamps with covered lamp shades. I felt like I was in a speakeasy, but I guess that was the point.

While I was disappointed I hadn't been able to snag a cool outfit from the closet, I had made do in a very thin white leather shirt slash jacket and a diaphanous layered lilac skirt that was from agnès b. like twenty years ago. I had also splurged on cool dangling earrings from an up-and-coming designer in NoLita.

Gabe and I had just finished singing "Happy Birthday" to Teagan over the DJ's remixes when Gabe's jaw dropped as he grabbed my arm.

"Okay, ten o'clock there is the hottest guy!" squealed Gabe.

"*Ten o'clock*? Where the hell is that?" asked Teagan, who was already a bit tipsy from the mojitos.

"Over there," said Gabe, abandoning his code and flagrantly pointing to a guy at the bar.

He *was* hot. He looked like Brad Pitt when he was still with Jennifer Aniston but right before their divorce, when he had that short cropped blondish haircut pre-*Troy*, but not as blond as it was when he was with Gwyneth Paltrow, and also about twenty years younger. And his clothes were cool, kind of black on black (shirt, pants) that were more thrown on than contrived to be a badass. Just as I was staring at him he turned and caught my eye and smiled, holding up his beer bottle as if to say "cheers."

"He just smiled at me! Oh my God, heart palpitations," said Gabe, fanning himself.

Wait, wasn't he smiling at me?

"Really?" I asked, confused.

"Go talk to him! Go talk to him!" commanded Teagan, waving her mini-drink-straw in the air. I stayed out of it.

"Should I?" asked Gabe, turning and stealing a glance at the guy again.

"Totally!" urged Teagan.

Gabe took a swig of his drink and got up, emboldened. I watched him walk over to the Brad Pitt guy and say something. God, this was either going to be amazing for Gabe or really mortifying. I saw Gabe throw his head back and laugh, then point to our table, put his hand on Brad Pitt's, really flirty, then guide him toward us. So I was wrong. He *had* smiled at Gabe. But as Gabe sat down, his eyes widened.

"Guys, this is Matt," said Gabe.

"Hey," said Matt, staring at me as I greeted him. Up close he looked less like Brad but was still *gorgissimo*. He had amazing hazel eyes, with brown and green flecks. "Mind if I join you?"

He slid into the booth without waiting for our response.

"So Matt here is drowning his sorrows cause he just broke up with his *girlfriend*," said Gabe, enunciating the last word.

Girlfriend? So I was right! Ha.

"So I told him he had to come over to our table right away if he wanted to be cheered up. He thought I was hitting on him, silly boy, but I told him I was sitting with two very lovely ladies," said Gabe quickly.

"And he was right," said Matt, again staring at me.

"Great, well, nice to meet you," I said.

"So what's your number, Matt?" asked Teagan bluntly.

Instead of being put off by her brusque manner, Matt smiled. "My number? Eleven."

I laughed and Gabe giggled.

"Seriously, I just graduated from Georgetown, headed to law school in the fall, and am taking the summer off. I did some traveling for two months, and now I'm just hanging."

"Where are you going to law school?" I asked. Columbia, please!

"Harvard?" he said, as if he wasn't sure I'd heard of it.

95

"Why is it that people who go to Harvard always say it like it's a question? Harvard? Do you know it?" said Teagan, mocking him.

But Matt laughed in agreement. "You're right, so lame." Then he deepened his voice dramatically. "I'm going to Harvard."

I liked a guy who had a sense of humor about himself.

"That's better," said Teagan.

"Now tit for tat. Tell me who you guys are and what you're doing here," he said, looking at me again.

We spent the next forty-five minutes downloading our lives and filling him in on *Skirt* and the recent Daphne debacle. Matt listened intently and laughed at all the right places. He even offered relationship advice to Gabe, who was bemoaning the lack of male attention. That was cool. So often straight guys are totally squeamish and immature when it comes to gay men. But Matt seemed not to care that Gabe was gay, earning bonus points in my book. By the end of the conversation, Matt was even pointing out potential suitors to Gabe, which had us all in fits of laughter.

Later, Teagan and Gabe got up to dance, and Matt and I were left alone.

"Your friends are funny," he said.

"I know," I said. I had *really* lucked out with these roomies.

"Do you want to dance?" he asked. Wow. Bold! I got a wave of that nervous excitement when you know someone seems into you. Too bad I sucked at dancing.

"I'd love to, but I'm inept," I said.

"Come on," he said. "No one is worse than me."

"Alright," I said, finally agreeing.

He was right about being a pretty bad dancer, but actually I didn't care, because before long we weren't really dancing, just kind of swaying closely for what seemed like hours. When Gabe and Teagan decided they'd had enough, we all left together. It was kind of a shock to be out on the street after so many hours in the dark club. Teagan and Gabe walked a bit ahead of us toward the subway, and Matt put his arm around me.

"So can I call you?" asked Matt at the subway steps.

"Sure," I said, scribbling my number on a scrap piece of paper. Butterflies!

"Great," he said, leaning in to give me a small kiss on my lips. A perfect kiss, not too long, not too short, but lip to lip. I slept very well.

Chapter Seventeen

I bounded out of bed and to my clothing rack outside my door. I might as well have had a soundtrack with "Joy to the World" playing along with my every move. It's funny how a new iron in the romance fire can fuel happiness. The crappy things seemed to go away—the stifling city heat didn't bother me, the subway seemed less stinkified, the crowded elevator ride up to work less claustrophobic.

When I got to my little veal-fattening pen (i.e., teeny tiny cubicle), I saw Daphne saunter by *avec* entourage, and even she didn't bother me. She passed by my desk without saying hi, and I didn't even think *bitch* or *clam*, just *MattMattMattMattMatt*.

"Hey, Kira," Alida said, rapidly approaching me. "Can I ask a favor? I'll tell CeCe I needed you—"

"Sure," I said, brightening at the chance to work with her. I was getting a burning sensation in my ear from spending every morning booking hair and makeup teams to go to Genevieve's and CeCe's respective abodes to beautify them for their nightly dinner parties. All the top editors had me do this, and it got really tiresome to coordinate. Especially when they'd fight over who got to use this or that hair stylist. There was no way to win.

"Great. You're not going to believe this," Alida said, leaning in to me. "Genevieve's new stepdaughter just got an assistant job down at *Tinsel Monthly*, and Genevieve said she can't dress. So now she's asked me, senior editor here, to pull five outfits a week to lend to the girl so she doesn't reflect poorly on Genevieve. I mean, God forbid she have an off-fashion day!" I could tell Alida thought Genevieve (a) sucked for wanting to make over this girl, and (b) double sucked for making a top fashion editor deal with the dumb task. I would have been furious, too. I felt good that Alida confided her obvious annoyance to me.

"You have great style and totally get it," Alida said to my glowing, pride-filled face. "Can you take over this project for me?"

"Absolutely. Consider it done," I assured her.

An hour later in the closet, I'd pulled a few options and was having fun accessorizing them when my phone buzzed. Could it be Matt already? My whole bod froze as I nervously fumbled to open my phone.

"Hello?" I said in an almost-whisper.

"Kira, hey, are you in a library or something? It's Matt. I was hoping we could hang out tonight."

Chapter Eighteen

*W*hen I emerged from the subway on Eighty-sixth and Lexington, I realized that except for the quick jaunt to Daphne's friend's parents' apartment for the lame-o party, I had not spent any time uptown at all. And that was a mistake, because even though downtown was cool and edgy and midtown was fun and business, uptown was so clean and orderly. I walked along Park Avenue, taking in all the grand limestone buildings with their sleek awnings and uniformed doormen opening the heavy latticed doors for well-dressed residents, and sighed. It would really be nice to have money and live here one day. All of the buildings had neat little flower boxes and gated trees so that dogs couldn't do their *bidniss* on them. And although the pulsing hip factor of downtown wasn't there, the stylish pedestrians were just as intriguing to me.

I supposed I was looking at everything with an extra spring in my step because I was on my way to meet Matt. He'd asked me on a real date to dinner at "his parents' favorite restaurant," and when I ran the name and address by Richard, he'd raised his eyebrows and told me it was "*très* swanky" and I "must have landed a rich pup." I felt like I was in the movies! Here I was in New York City, working at my dream job, and about to go out with "a rich pup" to a "swanky" restaurant. It was amazing!

When I found my way to Vico, a sleek-looking Italian restaurant with a clubby atmosphere, I scanned the room as I gave my name to the maître d'. Unfortunately, there was no sign of Matt yet. I didn't want to be the first one, and had purposely dragged my feet a little so I wouldn't come off like an eager beaver. But being prompt is not a crime.

The maître d' didn't find my name or Matt's, which was weird, but shrugged and said they had a table anyway, and led me to the back corner of the room. Right away a busboy rushed over and filled my water glass and another brought a bread basket. Then a waiter asked if I would like flat or sparkling water and seemed perplexed when I asked what was the difference between those and the one that the waiter had just poured for me. (He patiently explained that I was drinking tap water, which I suppose was just fine by me.) It was strange to be at a grown-up place like this without my parents, but then again, I couldn't even picture my parents here. We go out to dinner frequently, but to places like Houston's or the Cheesecake Factory. Sure, we've gone to Montello's, a little Italian place near our house, which has great food, but it's not really fancy seeing as they still give you crayons to draw on the paper tablecloths.

I scanned the menu as I waited for Matt. I couldn't believe the prices and I hoped (read: prayed) that he didn't expect us to split dinner. Luckily I had cash on me, but if we ordered first and second courses, it would be about one hundred dollars, which was way too exorbitant for me. The minutes ticked by, and I nervously kept sipping my water. The busboy kept coming up and refilling it, and the waiter asked me twice if I was sure I wouldn't like something to drink. It felt weird to order without Matt, but I finally broke down and ordered a Coke and the waiter seemed a little disappointed. Just as I was starting to panic, Matt arrived.

He smiled at me and waved, and my heart did a little dance. As he walked up the steps toward me, I noticed that he was wearing if not the same, then nearly identical black pants and shirt that he wore when I met him. Maybe that look was his thing.

"Hey, I'm so sorry I'm late," said Matt.

"No problem," I assured him.

"The good news is that I'm late for a reason," Matt said, grabbing a bread roll and breaking it in half. "I just nailed down my spring internship, and I am happy to say you're looking at Justice Ruth Bader Ginsburg's newest employee."

"No way! That is so major!"

"I know. Of course, I'm not her employee, just her unpaid intern, and the lowliest at that, but this is one of my lifelong dreams."

"I am so impressed," I said. Wow, this guy was going places! How did I luck out?

"But anyway, sorry to talk about me straight off the bat. Tell me about you and your day," he said, putting his hand on mine. I think I melted into the table.

"Um, well, it's not been as exciting as yours, that's for sure. I booked some foot models for our October pedicure article and had to rearrange some shelves, but that is so petty compared to what you're going to do." For the first time I felt like fashion was insignificant and lame. I aspired to write articles on shoes, and Matt aspired to change our country. I was so not worthy.

"Don't be crazy," scolded Matt. "Fashion and other leisure pursuits are just as vital as the judicial system. We need a little froth and fun in our life also, don't we?"

And with that, he had me. I looked at his eyes, which were sparkling in the dimly lit room, and knew then and there that Matt was special. He was not some fumbling lacrosse-stick-toting high school boy: He was a man.

As the dinner wore on (Matt told me to order "anything I want" and I did make a pig out of myself with the artichoke salad and homemade gnocchi), I learned that he grew up in New York but had gone to boarding school in Massachusetts at Holt Academy (which even I had heard of, seeing as it produced four U.S. presidents and was one of the toniest schools in the country), before going to Georgetown. He was a black diamond skier and a big mountain biker but didn't seem to care that I was hopeless with sports. The weird thing was that we had so much in common! I told him my favorite movie was *Rear Window* and he was stunned and told me it was his also! We both loved van Gogh and loathed modern architecture, and when I ordered tiramisu for dessert, his jaw dropped and he told me that it was his favorite dessert in the world. I wanted to get down on my knees and thank the stars for sending us both to Melt the same night.

I had thought I was so into James, but the more I got to know Matt, the more he seemed like my kind of guy. James was amazing, but he was obviously uncomfortable with the fact that both his dad and stepfather were wealthy and extremely successful. On the flip side, Matt casually told me that he had been really fortunate to grow up with extreme wealth, and rather than be all spoiled bratty about it, he planned to use his good fortune and education to change the policy of the U.S. government toward welfare recipients. How cool was that?

"I'm so glad I met you, Kira," said Matt after we finished the last dollop of mascarpone cream from our dessert.

I think I turned bright red. "I am, too."

"Can I get you anything else?" asked the waiter, approaching our table.

"We're all set," said Matt.

"Very well then," said the waiter, placing a leather-bound case with the bill on the edge of the table.

Matt glanced up at the waiter. "Oh, I'm charging it to my dad. Cal Rubin."

"You're Mr. Rubin's son?" asked the waiter.

"Yeah, Dad said just charge it to his house account. And add twenty-five percent for gratuity."

The waiter looked pleased. "Thank you so much, sir."

"No problem," said Matt, returning his gaze to me. "Shall we go on a walk?"

"Sure," I said.

Matt slid back my chair and we exited onto Madison Avenue.

"Let's take Fifth, much more scenic," said Matt, steering me down Ninety-third Street.

"I thought your last name was Hoffer," I said, confused.

Matt sunk his hands into his pockets. "It is. Cal Rubin is my stepdad, but he's like a dad to me."

"Oh," I said. It was weird that both James's and Matt's parents were divorced. All of my friends' parents at home were still married. I guess that wasn't the norm in Manhattan.

We turned onto Fifth Avenue and Matt pointed out the sights, my own personal tour guide. We passed the Jewish Museum, the Convent of the Sacred Heart, and then the Cooper-Hewitt Museum, which used to be Andrew Carnegie's mansion. All of the meticulously restored old buildings were gorgeous. It was such a nice night, with a warm breeze, to be walking around, and even though it was about nine o'clock, it still wasn't dark. People were spilling out of the park—joggers, bikers, and other couples like us. It was all so romantic.

When we got to about Eighty-fourth Street, Matt stopped in front of an ornate limestone building. The immaculately clad doormen stood at their posts outside as if royalty lived inside the gilded doors.

"Is something wrong?" I asked, noticing his fallen face.

"Yeah, sorry," he said, his voice tight.

"What?" I asked, concerned.

"It's just . . . this is my dad's building, and um, I don't get along with my stepmother," he lamented, looking up at the giant windows of the enormous apartments above. "When I pass it, it conjures up all these bad memories, 'cause basically I never see my dad because of my stepmonster and their new kids."

"Oh my God! That's horrible. I'm so sorry," I said, putting a hand on his arm to try to comfort him.

Matt suddenly shrugged, then smiled at me, taking my hand. "Kira, you're a really sweet girl. I'm so glad I met you."

He leaned down and delicately kissed my hand, which made me shiver, feeling like some cherished Victorian woman in a costume drama. He looked up and saw my smile, then swiftly pulled me into him and kissed me passionately. I wanted to melt— and not because of the warm summer night.

Before heading back uptown, Matt walked me all the way down to my apartment, which was like five miles, stopping to kiss me almost every block. I had never been happier to see so many red lights.

Chapter Nineteen

*W*hat came next was an Academy Awards–style montage of burgeoning romance, complete with Central Park smooches, sunsets by Chelsea Piers, and hand-holding down little winding streets. Matt would pick me up from *Skirt*, where I was still busting my hump working late, but his cute perch in the lobby made it all worth it. Within ten days, I felt like he was my full-out boyfriend! He started spending the night in our apartment every night, and while I hadn't given up the V-card, I knew he was the one I'd sleep with first. Definitely by summer's end.

During my CeCe servitude, my only bright moments were times plopped in Richard's office or when James and I would have the occasional chat in the hall. He was always so sweet, but not like Matt, who was so demonstratively attentive and, unlike James, clearly into me. Meanwhile, in my cinematic whirlwind, I oddly found that I didn't quite have everyone's approval on the new amore. Gabe, naturally, was as over the moon and was living vicariously through every kiss or inhalation of the fragrant flowers Matt brought me almost every day. He'd gush about how hot Matt was, how charming, how perfect. Teagan, however, was far less effusive.

"Are you, like, not into Matt?" I boldly asked one morning after Gabe gushed and she sat silent.

A shrug was her response. "He's okay, I guess."

Huh? Just *okay*? He was a prince! A chivalrous gent of yesteryear!

"Why aren't you into him?" I asked casually, trying to tone down my defensiveness.

"I don't know." She shrugged. "I mean, he's perfect. On paper," she said, cautiously. "But something about him seems a shade . . ." her voice trailed off.

"A shade what?" I probed.

"A shade shady."

Matt? Jealous, much? "I don't see it," I replied flippantly, and grabbed my bag to leave for work.

As I waited for them in the lobby, I just knew Teagan and Gabe were still in the kitchen talking about me, but I didn't really care. Sometimes I thought Teagan had to ruin everyone else's happiness. I mean, she almost seemed to gloat that she was right about Daphne getting the internship, and now she was probably just so envious that Matt went for me that she'd search for any excuse to hate him.

"Kira, no offense, okay?" said Teagan when she and Gabe emerged downstairs.

"Whatever, Teagan," I said, not looking at her. I pushed open the front door.

"Snippy!" Teagan muttered behind me.

I didn't even humor her with a response and refused to talk to her the entire subway ride. She didn't exactly try to talk to me, either. Gabe nervously maintained a monologue about celebrity gossip and other vapid topics the entire way to break the ice.

When we got to *Skirt*, the staff was gathering in the conference room for their weekly meeting. Alida had requested that the interns come to the first five minutes for some important announcement, and then we were to make ourselves scarce.

I sat down in the back corner, and James quickly slid into the seat next to me.

Although I was in the throes of my affair with Matt, I had to admit that I still kind of felt something for James. It had been sweet of him to defend me to Daphne that day—more than sweet. Sexy. Hot. Confident. But now that I was with Matt, I really wanted to move away from viewing him as a potential love interest, which he obviously was not, and try to view him as just a friendly colleague.

"Hey, Kira!" he whispered as Alida walked up to the head of the table. "Would you want to come with me to this Hockney lecture at the Whitney tonight? I have an extra ticket—"

I started to flush with excitement until I remembered Matt.

"Oh, thanks, James," I responded. "I can't. I have—I'm busy, actually. But thanks, anyway. I love Hockney." It sounded like a cool event, but Matt was going to take me out to Klimt, a new Austrian restaurant in Tribeca.

"Oh. Okay. Another time, then," he said.

"Okay, people, simmer," ordered Alida. "So, as some of you know, Genevieve, aside from being editor in chief, also works tirelessly for the Fashion and Design Institute at the Manhattan Museum of Art, and their annual ball—which is *the* party of the year—is on Friday. Mr. Hughes has generously taken an extra table this year and so we are inviting the interns to attend."

"Provided that you all work through the cocktail hour checking people in," added Genevieve. She was a woman of few words, but whatever she tersely said had a strong effect.

Even though we had to work, there were gasps of delight from all of us. This event was profiled not only in every magazine—Hughes-owned or not—but also on television channels and newspapers around the world. It was attended by Hollywood stars, top fashion designers, and other luminaries who wanted to see and be seen.

"In addition," Alida added, "you are each allowed to bring one guest." Squeals of delight. I hoped Matt would be free.

The rest of the day was nonstop craziness as I finished my travails for CeCe, helped Richard with his files, and popped by Alida's office to see if she needed anything. Her intern had left already (at the stroke of five, natch), so she took me up on my offer to be of assistance. I knew Matt wasn't picking me up at home until eight o'clock, so I had plenty of time.

"So Kira," Alida asked as I sorted new threads, Polaroiding them and placing them in fall shoot files while she answered e-mails, "tell me, do you see yourself working in magazines?"

"Oh yes," I gushed. "I love it here. I mean, granted, I'm total Xerox girl, but I feel like I am soaking up so much."

"And what if you were ever an editor . . ." she looked at me curiously. "What would you do? What would you want to add?"

"*Me?*" I was surprised she'd even care what a lowly worker bee like moi would ever think. As much as I thought Alida and I connected, I still felt like a mannequin with hands for snapping Polaroids, not a thinking human.

"Well, I'd do a lot," I started cautiously as she looked at me. "I would really sharpen the tone of the writing, give it that voice— it used to be snarkier, you know, kind of witty, tight, funny. Um . . . I'd overhaul some of the graphics, make them bolder, darker, edgier. Maybe experiment with more vintage looks like Warholian silkscreen images, chunky lettering, collages, things that lend energy. You know, that make every page pop. I like to turn the page and have everything be eye-catching and bold," I finished, thinking maybe I'd ranted too much. I was letting my imaginary corner office eclipse reality.

"Interesting," she said with a smile. "Good to know."

"I'm really excited for the big FDI event," I said, revved up. "I'm bringing this new guy I met recently."

"Oh *really*?" Alida asked with Richard-style taunting. "Can't wait to meet him!"

"I'm actually meeting him for dinner tonight—" I said, checking out the clock. It was still only seven.

"Go, go, go!" Alida said. "A gal's gotta primp. I'll take over and see you tomorrow."

"Are you sure?" I asked. I didn't want to leave her with more work.

"Totally," she said sternly. "Have a blast."

At the elevator, I found James waiting as well. "Hi, what time's your lecture?" I asked.

"In about twenty minutes. I'm just going to hop on the bus. Hopefully there will be one."

"I'm sad to miss it," I said as we boarded the surprisingly empty elevator. James got on and pressed the button, brushing against me ever so slightly.

He looked at me carefully. "What, you got a hot date?"

I couldn't decipher his tone. It was even, but not without emotion.

"Actually, yes," I said, turning a little red despite myself.

James's eyebrows shot up and his mouth tightened. "Really?"

"Yup," I said weakly. It was weird to talk to James about this. I felt . . . like I was cheating on him? No, that was dumb. I was sort of embarrassed. I didn't know why. I liked Matt, and I was into him, but for some odd reason I felt like I was betraying James a bit. Which was insane! We had only had a relationship in my mind.

"I'm jealous," said James.

"What?" I sputtered. "You are?"

James looked straight into my eyes as I felt my knees grow weak. It was definitely a moment, and I thought he would say something, but then the elevator stopped and a woman got on, ruining everything. He watched the woman furiously press the lobby button three times, and then he turned back to me with a smile.

"Of course," he said, now playful. "I want to make sure my friends are going out with nice guys. You'll have to bring him around so I can grill him."

"Oh, okay," I said.

The moment was broken. When we parted ways, I felt a weird dizzy strangeness, wondering if that really happened or if I was just making it up. But I put it out of my mind as I raced home to primp.

As soon as I got to the apartment, I dove into the shower. Shoot. Fifteen minutes to dry my hair, pick out a killer outfit, and put on makeup. After a racing whirlwind to get ready, I'd pulled it off. It was 8:05. Then 8:15. Then 8:30. Where was Matt? Finally, at 9:15, Teagan and Gabe came home from shooting pool at a hall in the East Village.

"Whatcha doin' here, girl?" Gabe asked, looking at my gussied-up self, all dressed with no place to go.

"Matt didn't come or call," I lamented. "I'm really bummed."

"Kira," began Teagan.

"You know what, Teagan? Your thoughts about Matt are really not helpful," I said. Why did she have it out for Matt? No need for lemon juice in my emotional paper cut.

"Okay, sorry, I won't give you my two cents," said Teagan, heading off to her room.

"Thanks," I said. I didn't need her two cents if they made me feel like one cent.

"Don't worry, honey, he must've got laid up. A mellow night in will do you some good," said Gabe, hugging me.

By eleven, I was in pj's, face washed, still bewildered, when my cell rang. It was Matt, apologizing profusely. He'd bumped into an old friend from Holt Academy and then he tried to call me but his phone battery died, and he was incredibly sorry but wanted to make it up to me. After being so excited and then so let down, I was at least happy to know he was (a) alive and (b) still into me, so I brushed off my annoyance and asked him to come to the FDI event with me.

"But you have to show up on time to the event, Matt," I said. "It's part of my job."

"Don't worry, Kira, I'll be there," he promised. "Sleep tight."

Chapter Twenty

*T*he grand glass-ceiling ballroom of the Manhattan Museum of Art was of gargantuan proportions. Urns the size of Olympians were overflowing with white flowers as lighting technicians dangled from thirty-foot-high poles, installing just the right scheme of hues to make the beautiful people look even more beautiful. Gabe, Teagan, and I had all come straight to the ballroom that morning as instructed, with our gowns (borrowed from the fashion closet with permission) in garment bags, which we stowed in the coat check. There was so much to be done—I couldn't believe the stark hall would be transformed in eight hours into a lavish, petal-covered, luxurious ball for the crème de la crème to air kiss, clink glasses, and dance the night away.

First Alida had us sit with the event planner, Langley Veer de Veer, to double check that all the seating cards, table assignments, and place cards matched up—a nightmare would be to have an advertiser arrive to their assigned table only to find there was no place for them. So I went over the list three times with a fine-tooth comb with Cecilia, who was also assigned to the task. We were courteous to each other, and although I should maybe have been a little harsher considering she and Jane dropped me like a hot potato when Daphne had moved on from me, right now I didn't care. I had a newfound confidence with Matt. Before I knew it, Cecilia had disappeared like the wind. It figured.

Gabe was laying out the cards, each fresh from the on-site calligrapher's pen, in alphabetical order on a bed of giant peonies. Twenty florists from Veer de Veer's design team labored on every centerpiece as two thousand votives were placed around the room, illuminating the space with a warm and radiant glow.

Next the slipper chairs were brought in with their custom upholstered cushions, and Gabe and I tied a half-yard of chocolate brown velvet ribbon around each linen napkin.

It was magical watching the whole thing come together. Not even in the wedding pages of *Town & Country* or *InStyle* had I seen such an opulent affair. It was what I imagined ragers at

Versailles to be. And then some.

Finally, as every minute detail came together before our very eyes, it was time to quickly change so we could assume our places checking in guests as they climbed from their limos onto the red carpet. *Skirt* had taken over the back section of the museum to use as a makeshift dressing room. I unzipped the garment bag with excitement; this was the first time in my life that I would don a dress by a *real* designer. Trixie had helped me pick out the gorgeous emerald-blue strapless Rochas dress and had lent me divine silver Sergio Rossi heels from his personal collection. (I wondered what Sergio Rossi did with his personal collection of high heels, but never mind.) I felt like a princess. I mean, Jennifer Aniston had worn *this very dress* on our June cover, and now I was wearing it! And it was, like, twenty-five thousand dollars to boot!

Richard sweetly handed me some gorgeous Temple St. Clair earrings that he had "borrowed" from the accessories closet and adjusted the hem of my skirt before pronouncing me "gorge" and rushing off. Although Teagan and I were not really talking, we were still cordial, and I was grateful when she offered her perfume bottle. I nervously sprayed some as a final touch.

I took my place with Gabe and Teagan behind the table, which was covered with a stunning embroidered lace cloth and sheets of paper with every guest's name. One by one they entered like swans, fluttering and preening, every hair in place, every diamond shining, every stitch of clothing immaculate.

After most of the arrivals had teetered off and Alida told us that we could go to our table, in waltzed Daphne. Miss Hughes, who had been absent from the preparations all day, was in haute couture from Dior and had clearly been at a salon to get her chignon that perfect. She wore a small delicate diamond comb in her updo, and casually held what I recognized as a Van Cleef & Arpels vintage diamond *necessaire* clutch. Behind her were Jane and Cecilia, both in equal photo-ready form. So that's where Cecilia went. I should have known the Trumpettes would skip the toils of preparation only to arrive fully glossed while we were left to shove a brush through our locks under the fluorescent lights of the museum bathroom.

After another stream of various boldfacers, in walked James, and I did a double take. I was used to seeing him in T-shirts and other casual fare, so it was a shock to see him wearing proper black tie, and I have to say it looked amazing. I loved it when men wore the old classic tuxedos and loathed how most of Hollywood felt the need to jazz up their suits. Did they think it was edgier? Why mess with something that works? But James clearly didn't feel the need to do anything, and the result was perfection.

"Kira," he said, coming up to our check-in table. "You look . . . really beautiful—" There was such sincerity in his earnest expression, I was extra struck by his compliment.

Before I could answer, Alida interrupted.

"Kira! Hi, I need you to come with me to help with the back door," said Alida, harried and flustered. "Selma Blair's limo is at the back, and I need you to guide her through to the cocktail reception." I got up, giving James a "what can I say?" look, and followed her obediently. Selma Blair? I could never have imagined that I would be meeting celebrities! And she turned out to be so sweet, although I was too starstruck to make any real conversation.

Next I helped usher guests from the reception into the main hall, which by this point was so beautiful with the bursting peonies and flickering candles that I couldn't wait to see Matt and have a dance with him. Where was Matt? I wasn't wearing a watch, but I knew that it had to be past the appointed hour. I hoped that he was already here somewhere, but as I made my way through the crowd and past the waiters serving hors d'oeuvres, I couldn't find him.

After an interminable cocktail hour (during which time I went to the front entrance three separate times to see if Matt had arrived), we took our seats. Our interns' table was miles away from the dance floor.

Just as we were sitting down, Daphne arrived holding her table forty-seven calligraphied place card. "*This* is table forty-seven?" she asked, aghast. "I can't believe it! I'm at the interns table?"

"Well, you are an intern," James said, sitting down with a smile. I was glad he was at our table. He didn't seem fazed by having to sit near his ex.

"And you're not. So why are you at our table?" snapped Daphne.

"I requested your table. I thought it would be more amusing."

I could tell that Daphne was seething. She kept looking around, craning her neck to see guests entering. I had been keeping my distance from her of late, which actually wasn't hard because she seemed like she was finally forced to do some work for once. Working for Genevieve was no joke. Daphne was constantly called out to greet every Tom, Dick, and Harry fashion person who came to see Genevieve, and it wasn't so glamorous fetching coffee for Kate Hudson or getting chicken nuggets for Colin Farrell. Sometimes I'd see Daphne sitting at her desk outside Genevieve's office and I actually felt bad for her. Just a little. No more long lunches with her friends—Cecilia and Jane would wave to her as they took off to La Goulue—and no more doing fun stuff like helping with the shoots or going through the cool new clothes. Daphne's gig was strictly clerical. And with two assistants above her, she was the low man on the totem pole.

That said, I still would have wanted the job. The access was undeniable. And I would want that feeling of winning, because that's what it was. Daphne and I were alike in that way: We had always won everything we wanted. I did it through hard work, and she did it through the lucky gene pool. But whatever. Let her have the job. She was still all fired up about her "responsibility" to find the person stealing clothes out of the closet, always making surprise cameo appearances to check on people in there (once erroneously accusing Trixie of stealing a vintage T-shirt, which, much to Daphne's embarrassment, turned out to be her own; Trixie produced the receipt), and talking loudly in the kitchen about what suffering would befall the person who was filching the goods. I wondered if Genevieve had made the whole thing up as a cruel joke just so she could sit back and watch Daddy's little girl eavesdrop on everyone and turn into the loathed office narc, but despite her knowledge of fashion, Genevieve didn't seem that clever to me. It was Alida, after all, who ghostwrote Genevieve's "Letter from the Editor."

In any event, Daphne mattered little to me now that our competition had ended.

In the meantime, I shook hands with Jane's and Cecilia's guests, wondering why Daphne hadn't invited anyone. She obviously wanted to be on the prowl. And with her heaving cleavage and piles of bling, I was sure she'd snag her fish of choice. I scanned the room before sitting down—still no sign of my date. The waiters had placed small salads in front of us with poached lobster and vinaigrette, and I didn't want him to arrive in the middle of dinner. The empty seat next to me felt like an elephant in the room, and when I glanced across the table, my eyes locked with Daphne's.

"So, Kira, where's your date?" asked Daphne with a raised brow. She was one down from me, seated on the other side of Matt's empty place.

"He's probably on his way," I said confidently.

"Late again?" Teagan asked. My blood boiled. How dare she!

And in front of *everyone?* But before I could say anything, I felt a hand on my bare shoulder.

"Sorry I'm late," Matt said, kissing my cheek and taking his seat. He looked a bit disheveled, hair slightly wet, coat unbuttoned, as if he had raced to get there. I was psyched to see that he was wearing a tuxedo but a little bummed that he had foregone the usual bow tie and chosen the more modern long black tie. I glanced at James's outfit with envy. Matt leaned in, gave me another kiss on my cheek, and whispered, "I wanted to look perfect for you." All of my anger melted. I shot a smug look at Teagan and then turned back to Matt, noticing Daphne staring at him with saucer eyes. *Cute, huh, Daph?*

Matt and I giggled over our first course, and I was thrilled to see Daphne checking him out slyly. I knew she wanted to get the four-one-one on him, but I hoarded him through the appetizer just to drive her a little crazy. When the time was right and he told her all about his life, she would be green with jealousy. It wasn't until the main course arrived, and I was forced into a dull conversation with Cecilia's boring boyfriend on my right, that Daphne got a chance to give Matt the inquisition. Where was he from? Where did he go to school? Oh really? *Holt Academy? Harvard in the fall?* As soon as she learned all the pertinent and impressive details, I saw her turn on her charm. That was it. It was grossing me out how obviously predatory she was about my date. I was just about to sharpen my cat claws when Alida summoned me.

"Kira," she said. "I need you to come help me with some press shots—"

I looked around the table, annoyed. On the one hand it was flattering that Alida had come to me for help, but on the other hand why did it seem like I was the only intern who was pulling my weight around here? The Trumpettes were being treated like guests of honor, and even Gabe and Teagan were laughing and refilling their champagne glasses, chatting away with a hot waiter from Pulp who Gabe had picked up the night before and asked to accompany him.

I wanted to respond, "No, Alida! It's not okay!" but instead I whispered to Matt that I would be right back and obediently followed and helped her corral various socialites for press shots for the four pages of party pictures we would be running.

It took forever, and let me tell you, these heels may be beautiful, but they were not meant to be worn. At least worn by someone who had to stand around pulling people into pictures and bending down to help socialites adjust their hems or pull up spaghetti straps. I know the deal was that we had to work to earn our keep there, but I was frustrated. I just wanted to get back to Matt and enjoy the party. It wasn't fair that I was the only one working! Out of the corner of my eye I saw Matt clearly charming everyone, including Daphne, who had her head thrown back in laughter as she delicately fingered a small diamond locket around her neck. She could have her heiress's choice and here she was, trying to lure my date!

124

As things started to wind down, I finally got back to my table, only to find Gabe, Teagan, and Gabe's date. "Where's Matt?" I asked.

"He, uh . . ." Gabe trailed off.

"He took a walk with Daphne," replied Teagan, not smugly, but sadly. "Sorry, Kira."

Chapter Twenty-One

"There you are!" I said, trying to be casual but fearing that my voice was betraying me.

"Hey," said Matt, with an expression I couldn't read. It was obvious, however, that Daphne was less than thrilled that I had found them. And boy had it taken a while. I had gone back and forth around the entire ballroom, upstairs to the painting exhibit, and had walked the long hallway with the early American folk art cases, only to discover Matt and Daphne sitting on a bench by the enormous floor-to-ceiling windows that looked out onto the museum's greenhouse.

I wanted to say, "What the hell were you thinking?" but instead I said, "The band is still playing. Any interest in heading downstairs?" It was important to play it cool. I didn't want Daphne to think I cared that she had absconded with my boyfriend. But what the hell was he thinking? He would bear my wrath when we were alone.

"Sure," said Matt.

"Let's go downstairs," said Daphne suddenly. "Derek Wombley—you know, the new Calvin Klein model? Well, he's been *begging* me to dance with him all night."

"Well, if *Derek Wombley* has been asking you to dance, we should really hurry," said Matt in a teasing tone.

Then he linked one of his arms with me and the other with Daphne and started running down the hallway. "Matt, stop! I can't run in these shoes!" I said, giggling.

Daphne was also running but finally yanked her arm from Matt's. "What are you doing?" she said harshly. "I don't want to ruin my outfit."

"Well, excuse me, Miss Magazine Heiress," teased Matt.

Daphne looked at me, who was laughing, and at Matt, who was waiting for her response. I could tell she was deciding whether or not to freak out or to laugh it off. She chose the latter.

"You are a madman, Matthew!" she said, straightening her dress and continuing on.

Matthew?

Matt and I followed her down the stairs, and when we returned to the ballroom, she immediately broke off from us and went in search of her male model. When she was distinctly out of earshot I turned to Matt.

"Why did you wander off with her? She's so lame," I said.

Matt looked at me and smiled. "Jealous?"

"No."

"Jealous!" said Matt, pulling me in for a hug.

"You've heard me talk about her, you know how I think she sucks," I said, not wanting to sound bitchy, but sounding bitchy.

"You were MIA for like an hour! What was I supposed to do?" asked Matt.

That was true. But still.

"Yeah, but why did you go upstairs?" I knew I sounded like a jealous girlfriend, but I didn't like the whole situation.

"Kira, don't get panicky. I wanted to get away from all these society people. They give me the heebie-jeebies. Like I said, there are a ton of my parents' friends here. So I asked Gabe if he wanted to check out the art and he was preoccupied with his new boyfriend, but Daphne volunteered. What could I do, say, 'No, you can't come?'"

Yes! "I guess not," I admitted. "Well, what did you talk about?" I asked as he grabbed my hand.

"You know, people we knew in common, boarding schools, country clubs, that sort of stuff."

"Oh," I said. For the first time I felt like it might be a problem that I was not from the fancy world that Matt and Daphne live in. But Matt read my mind.

"Listen, don't let your mind go crazy. Let's take off. I know you didn't get any dinner, so let's head over to Cipriani and have a late-night supper, okay?"

I smiled and nodded.

We had a great time at Cipriani. Until the bill came and Matt realized he'd forgotten his wallet and I had to pay for the dinner on the credit card my parents gave me for emergencies. I knew he would pay me back, but it was a stressful feeling, putting a two-hundred-dollar late-night snack on Dad's AmEx. I guess the theory that rich people never carry cash is true, as Matt never had any on him.

Matt stayed over again and things got even more hot and heavy than usual. I finally had to practically put a barrier between us. I wasn't exactly thrilled with him tonight—besides, I just wanted to wait. He seemed understanding, but slightly annoyed, and he rolled away without cuddling with me like usual. My fairy-tale evening had turned into a pumpkin.

Chapter Twenty-Two

The next day at work I felt hit by a cyclone as I was in the middle of an editor tug-of-war with three different people needing my help. Alida won out. I packed trunks for her big fall shoots in the Caribbean, Sicily, and Africa, and then reorganized her entire office before she sent me out to Top Shoe Repair to collect all the scuffed sandals from the last cover story.

When I returned to Alida's office, I heard Daphne's trademark coy giggles around the corner and was stunned to discover that the source of her mirth was none other than Matt.

"Look who I found in the lobby!" she exclaimed, looking at me with an arched brow.

"Surprise," said Matt, grinning. Jane and Cecilia sat nearby, watching.

"Oh . . . hi," I managed to sputter. "Um, what are you doing here?" I inquired as Daphne ran a bejeweled hand through her mane.

"I wanted to stop by and say hello," he said.

I was psyched that he came by, but I was an *intern*, so it wasn't encouraged to have drop-ins upstairs in the office. We usually met in the lobby. And it also felt odd that he had never asked to stop by before. Now that he knew Daphne, is that why he wanted to come? Maybe I was being paranoid. I mean, it was probably totally accidental that he ran into Daphne before me. But then why was he sitting there chatting with her and not putting out the Amber Alert to track me down?

"Hello," said James, walking by piled down with files. He glanced at me and Daphne and then stuck his hand out to Matt. "James. We met the other night."

"Yes, good to see you," Matt said casually, shaking his hand.

I saw Daphne roll her eyes at Cecilia and Jane, inferring that James's presence was unbearable. Suddenly a tsunami of tension rolled over us and we were mute for a good two seconds. Leave it to Daphne to pierce the silence with her confident chirp.

"So, you guys, we should all really hit Melt tonight—" she said, looking only at Matt. "MK and A will be there, and it should be an A-list night."

"Awesome," replied Matt. "Sounds like a plan."

A plan? A plan without consulting moi, his girlfriend, who was seriously considering laying down her virgin chips?

"Matt," I interrupted. "I thought we were going to see that motorcycle documentary at the Angelika."

"I heard that's really good," interjected James.

"Oh, right," Matt said, deflated. "Maybe another time—give the Olsens my best," he joked.

"Bummer," said Daphne. "Well, I have to get back to work. I have soooooo much to do. Genevieve's going to Paris next week and dining with Herr Lagerfeld. Craziness."

"Oh my God, you are like a workhorse," said Jane.

"I know. But it's my company one day, and I want it to run smoothly," said Daphne, turning on her heels.

Once she was gone, Jane and Cecilia immediately took off to get manis and pedis at Bliss, leaving me alone with Matt and James.

"Hey, Matt," James said. "The other night, I couldn't help but overhear you say you went to Holt Academy?"

"Yeah, that's right," Matt said.

"Mmm-hmm," James replied with furrowed brow. I wondered where this was going.

"I'm sure you've heard of it. We've produced tons of presidents."

"Right," said James. "Well, catch you later." He walked away giving me a look that I couldn't read.

Later that evening, Matt, Gabe, Teagan, and I were waiting in line for tickets at the famed art house theater when Matt started nervously patting his jacket pockets.

"Damn!" he muttered. "I left my wallet at home!"

It wasn't a problem, as I had just that morning taken two twenties out of my secret stash.

"Hakuna matata," I replied, passing the nose-pierced cashier the money. "I happen to have some Andrew Jacksons," I said. Matt leaned in to give me a kiss. Out of the corner of my eye I saw Gabe beaming, hand on heart, and Teagan, arms crossed. Maybe the reason she didn't like Matt was because her summer didn't spawn a New York romance like mine? Whatever the reason, her attitude was starting to bug me.

After the movie, we all went home to our pad, and Matt and I retreated to my room. There was no air conditioner, and on this particularly hot night, sweat covered us as we rolled atop my comforter. We were breathing twice as hard, not from our burning passion, but from the humid choking haze strangling the city.

He suddenly fumbled in his pocket, pulling out a condom from his Levi's.

"Kiiiira," he whispered, as if the letters of my name were honey dripping off a spoon. "I want you."

Talk about the heat of the moment. Truth be told, I wanted him, too. I felt ready, I think. Maybe it was the charge of testosterone or his impatience with me, but I suddenly got a wave of fear. Me. Miss bold and brassy was terrified. Not here. Not in this cot. Not with the thermometer mercury at equatorial levels. I was uncomfortable. So I stopped him.

"Oh, come on!" he said, rolling over in a huff.

"Matt—"

"Forget it, I'm tired."

The next morning he slept in as I tiptoed out to meet Gabe and Teagan to go to work. I sat mute on the train, heart pounding.

"What's up, buttercup?" Gabe asked, moving a piece of hair that was matted to my face. "You look like you just got shat out of a camel's ass."

Gee, thanks.

"I don't know . . ." I replied nervously, looking at Teagan, not wanting to fuel her fire. "I just . . . Matt and I almost did it last night and I just couldn't."

"Thank God," Teagan said, slurping her iced black coffee.

"Why do you have it in for him?" I blurted, annoyed.

"You told me you didn't want to hear my two cents," said Teagan.

"Do you actually have something to say, or are you just jealous that I have found someone and you haven't?"

Gabe's eyes moved back and forth between us as if he were at Wimbledon, but instead of a yellow ball, he was following harsh words between roommates.

"I knew you'd think that," said Teagan. "And that's really lame. I'm just looking out for your best interests."

"Oh? And what are my best interests?" I said, crossing my arms fiercely.

Teagan took a deep breath. "Kira, I am your friend, and I'm not trying to sabotage your relationship. Matt is sketchy. He's easy on the eyes, I'll admit that. But do not think for one second that he is worthy. Not of you. That first night we met him, I could have sworn I saw him take a twenty off the table when we were leaving. We had left the cash for the bar tab right under our drinks, remember? And as we were walking out, he slid the glass aside and took it."

"Why didn't you say something then?" I challenged.

"Because I wasn't sure."

"And now you are? I don't think he would have done that," I stated.

"Kira, haven't you noticed his wallet is always 'missing'? How you reach for your money constantly?"

"He pays for stuff all the time!" I responded, my brain immediately thinking of all the times *I* had to pay.

"Please. He crashes in our apartment, he eats our food, he networks with Daphne. The guy is a louse!"

I had it with her patronizing tone. Like she is Miss Relationship Queen.

"Whatever. I am so not dealing with this assault."

"You guys, stooop!" Gabe pleaded in a singsongy voice, but it was too late. When the subway hit our stop and the double doors slid open, I stormed off and hoofed it past them to work, leaving them both in the wake of my anger and confusion.

Chapter Twenty-Three

"Hey, Kira, can I talk to you?"

I looked up from my perch on the floor, where I was reorganizing the new batch of male model cards from Elite, to see James towering over me.

"Sure."

"Um, maybe not here," he said, glancing around the buzzing office. The Trumpettes were within earshot, so clearly whatever he wanted to say was for my ears only.

I followed him into Richard's office (he was in Brazil for the week, shooting Gisele) and James closed the door. I stared outside the windows—I had been trapped in the maze all morning and didn't even notice that it had started to drizzle. Suddenly the freezing air-conditioning, compounded with the wet view, gave me a chill. I regretted wearing my thin lilac blouse and short Milly skirt.

"Are you cold? Here," said James, taking off his sweatshirt and gallantly handing it to me.

"That's okay."

"No, come on. I insist."

I supposed I should say no and go borrow something from the closet (the new furs had arrived for the winter issue; shall I don a mink?), but I knew that lately every time I entered the closet it was under Daphne's watchful eyes. So I semireluctantly put on the sweatshirt, noticing that it smelled like James. I couldn't place the smell; it was more like soap and manliness, not cologne or anything like that.

"I wanted to talk to you about something, as a friend," began James, his eyes carefully locking on mine. I noticed that his hair had grown out a bit and it looked good the way it flopped around his ears.

"Sure," I said, suddenly nervous. Did he want to tell me that I had BO? That I was doing a sucky job? I normally wasn't paranoid, but he seemed so grave that I knew something major was up.

"It's about Matt."

"Oh."

"I know it's not my place, but I feel like you and I have become friendly, and friends look out for each other," he said, glancing down at the floor.

Friends look out for each other. Uh huh. I didn't say anything, so he continued.

"I don't know how to put this without sounding like an ass, but I think you should . . . watch out for him. Where did you meet him?"

"I met him at Melt," I said, slowly registering his words. "What do you mean 'watch out for him?'"

"Listen, I'm just gonna lay it on the line. I think the guy is, I don't want to say a con artist, because it's not Vegas or anything, but I don't trust him. I think he's a liar."

I felt my face begin to burn. "Why?"

"It sounds petty, but he said a few things to me that don't add up. He told me—and you heard it, I asked him again in front of you on purpose—that he went to Holt Academy. Thing is, it's called Holt School. Anyone who went there would know that."

"That seems kind of minor, James," I said defensively. So I was supposed to watch out for the guy over one little word choice?

"That's not all. He said other things. He told me his dad is Cal Rubin . . ."

"That's his *stepfather*," I interrupted.

"Right. But I know Cal Rubin. He doesn't have a son, or a stepson; he has a daughter, Alisa, who lives in London."

"Could be a different Cal Rubin."

"Look, Kira, I'm not trying to nail the guy. I just have this weird feeling. Have you ever met his parents?"

"No . . ."

"Been to his apartment?"

"No," I confessed. Suddenly it was like pieces of a giant jigsaw puzzle were coming together.

"Have you met his friends? Who was he with when you met him at Melt?"

"He was alone," I said quietly. "And I've never met his friends."

James nodded fiercely. "See, something doesn't add up. He name-drops all these schools and clubs and vacation places, but something seems a little off, like he *read* about them but never actually *went* there."

My mind started racing. I remembered that Matt had told Gabe that he went to La Coyote Resort in Mexico for spring break, but even Gabe knew that it had closed down a year ago. I hadn't thought twice about it and had shrugged it off, thinking he meant the year before. Now the fact that Matt almost always wore the same black clothes seemed suddenly important. And that he never had money on him. I was always paying for him, and now that I realized it, he never paid me back, even though he said he would. The only time he'd footed the bill was our first date . . . and that was a signature to his "stepdad's" account. Holy. Shit. But what did he think he could get from me? I wasn't rich, and he had to have figured that out by now.

James could tell I looked nauseous and put his arms on my

shoulders. "Look, don't worry. You weren't really serious with this guy, were you?"

I could only respond in the smallest voice. "No, not really."

But when I looked up at James, a single tear slid down my cheek. I was mortified. How could I have been so stupid? James pulled me close and gave me a hug.

"Don't worry, Kira. Look, the guy had everyone fooled. Look at Daphne; she's drooling after him now."

God, Daphne. *That's* why Matt was still hanging around. He knew he could use me to get to bigger prey. Matt must have set his sights on her because she had more money than me. Ugh. They deserved each other. Even though it was nice and cozy in James's embrace, I was still so super embarrassed that I wanted to get the hell out of there.

"Uh, thanks for the info, James, but I should bolt."

James gave me a strange look. I wiped the tear from my cheek and pulled myself together.

"Are you okay?"

"I'm fine, fine, thanks so much."

I turned and left the office. How humiliating! Of course it would work out that my first crush was the one to reveal that my boyfriend was a scam artist. Lovely. And to think I almost had sex with him! I wanted to puke. And loofah my body. My parents always said to be careful, be on guard with strangers, don't be so trusting—I had totally disregarded them and gotten sucked in.

I told CeCe that I thought I was getting the stomach bug,

and although she made me stand there for an additional twenty minutes on hold with the restaurant where she wanted to get a reservation, she finally released me. I took the subway home, getting drenched in the rain, climbed into my bed, and pulled up the covers.

After crying my eyes out, I drifted off to sleep.

Chapter Twenty-Four

*A*fter passing out in a shivering damp mass under my blanket, I finally came to a few hours later, feeling crushed by not only my blindness but also my acute guilt for freaking on Teagan. Here I had defended Matt tooth and nail only to discover that he was, in fact, a bona-fide scumbag. When I heard the door open, I staggered out, looking like a street urchin, to find Gabe and Teagan with Chinese takeout.

"Teagan," I said, gulping. "I owe you a mega-apology."

Even she looked surprised. "How come?"

My eyes started to well up. "Matt's a grifter."

I told them how James had shined the light on the narrow wormhole I'd been living in with my crush on Matt.

"Knock me over with a feather boa!" Gabe exclaimed, hand on heart. "I am in clinical shock! Somebody book me a suite at that *Girl, Interrupted* place! I am *freaking out!*"

"I'm sure you feel vindicated," I said to Teagan.

"Kira, I don't feel good about this. I'm sorry that it worked out this way. I really want you to have a nice boyfriend and be happy," she proclaimed, hugging me. Teagan, the self-professed hater of physical contact, actually initiated an embrace.

"Sorry I doubted you—" I said, hugging her back.

Gabe just stood there, still reeling.

"Gabe? Gaaabe!" Teagan teased. "Earth to you! What, a hot guy can't be a raging jerk-off?"

"No, I just, I just—"

"He's charming, right?" I asked him, wanting backup. Clearly I wasn't the only one sucked in by his alluring wiles.

"He's goooood," Gabe said, nodding slowly, still in space. "He's really good."

"So," Teagan said, putting a strong hand on my shoulder. "What are we gonna do about it?"

"What do you mean?" I asked, my eyes twinkling with thoughts of him being cuffed and collared. "Like, as in revenge?"

"As in, I say we take you out and cheer you up after we scarf this lo mein. We'll hatch our plan on the town!"

* * *

Two hours later, the three of us were full of MSG and dancing our hearts out at a hole-in-the-wall East Village club called Saint. Gabe was in heaven, as the room was packed with the most gorgeous gay guys I had ever seen.

"A far cry from East Jesus, Texas, or wherever it is you hail from," Teagan teased, winking at him as, mouth agape, he stared at the shirtless hotties.

We had finally collapsed into a corner booth and were refueling on Cokes and peanuts.

"I don't ever want to go home," Gabe said.

While I just had my own experience of how the big city can wake up the naive with a smack, Gabe had a wake-up call of his own: that this hot-blooded, electric Gotham was the first place that had made him feel whole. All summer he had seemed so happy and in his element, but I could tell of late he was getting progressively stressed about the end-of-summer discussion that he planned to have with his parents.

"Guys, my parents are coming next week. I have to tell them everything!" said Gabe.

"Do you think they'll freak?" I asked. Gabe was so sweet, I couldn't imagine that his parents were the type of people who would disown him or anything like that.

"I have no idea what they'll think."

"Are you more worried about telling them that you're gay or that you're not going to college back home?" I asked.

"Well, first off my dad will definitely have a hissy if I don't go to U of W. It's gonna be like dropping a bomb on them. My dad and his dad both played ball there and all that dumb crap. But helloooo? That's clearly not happening," he said, flexing a nonexistent bicep.

"Ain't that the truth." Teagan laughed. "The only balls flying at your face come in pairs!"

"As for the gay thing . . . I don't know. I'm hoping they have some inkling and it's not a total shock attack."

"Gabe, with those electric blue leg warmers and leopard shirts you don, I'm sure that they have some idea," said Teagan.

"You're right! But I'm scared. I need help!" said Gabe, his eyes pleading.

For the next hour we plotted how Gabe could break the news to his family. After deciding honesty was always the best policy and that he should just rip the proverbial Band-Aid off when they arrived, we focused our group's attention on the other dilemma du jour: Matt. Between shifts on the dance floor, we caucused and emerged at three A.M. with spirits high, ears still buzzing, and an ace up my sleeve.

Chapter Twenty-Five

"Hi, Matt, where are you?" I asked, walking along Seventy-second Street and Central Park West.

"I'm in the park at Seventy-second Street," he said. "Counting down 'til I can see you, beautiful. Where're your coordinates?"

"Oh, I'm a few blocks away," I lied, fighting fire with fire. "I'll meet you by the Bethesda Fountain."

I approached the park, catching him in my sights but always staying a few steps behind to spy on him. Turning the tables empowered me, and made me feel like he was the prey this time.

Fine, he was cute, but now, after everything, I thought he looked almost too hot, like a fake soap star. I wanted to watch him for a few minutes to see him in action. Was he like a predator, looking at girls to see who his next victim would be? No, not so far.

But then: There it was. When no one was looking, he casually bent down over the John Lennon memorial circle and picked up one of the many bouquets of flowers. And then I knew. Every time he brought roses for me, they'd been snatched from that monument for the dead Beatle. That little turd.

I arrived at Bethesda Fountain, practically gagging that I'd let this scumbag, this manipulative centipede, burrow into my life so deeply. But with Meryl Streep's aplomb, I brightened when I saw him and gave him a quick peck on the cheek.

"These are for you," he said, handing me the pilfered buds. "How's my girl?"

I could have said I was terrible, considering I had been fooled by a con artist, but I contained it. My roommates and I decided that if I called him out on his various falsehoods that he'd just walk off and do it again to some other unsuspecting fool. And why do that when we had a perfect one lined up for the taking?

"Listen, Matt—" I said, knowing full well any sentence that began with "look" or "listen" meant the relationship was going the way of the *Titanic*. "I've been thinking—"

"Is everything okay, sweetness?" he purred, stroking my cheek.

"You know, this is all happening so fast and to be totally honest, while I think you're great, I feel that I need to focus on work stuff. I'm not in a good place for a relationship right now. It's not you—it's me," I said, almost stifling a cackle.

Considering I'd just lobbed the most insulting breakup initiative ever—the "it's not you, it's me" refrain—he was taking it quite well. He didn't seem to care at all, in fact.

I continued. "I need to stay on my work path right now and I'm starting fresh at school next month—"

"Hey, sweetheart, I totally understand," he said soothingly, giving me a hug. Gee, that was easy. "I hope we can stay friends. No hard feelings."

"No."

A calmer breakup had never occurred in history, and as he walked off among the sunny crowds of park revelers, with his stolen "Imagine" flowers, I was happy to have him out of my life.

Chapter Twenty-Six

I tried to lay as low as humanly possible the next week at work for fear I would run into James. I know it's silly; he couldn't have been nicer, but I felt like such a complete nerd that I didn't want his sad looks of pity. I had slipped into his office early one morning and returned his sweatshirt with a little thank-you note pinned to it, and now, instead of being my usual run-around-Sally-how-can-I-help-you gal at the office, I mostly stuck to CeCe's lair. She had me doing totally boring stuff, like picking up plane tickets from the in-house travel agency and messengering them to the models, photographers, and makeup teams that were going on various shoots in Cabo, Paris, and Hawaii. She also had me create a master list of what models were affiliated with what cosmetic companies so we could pretend that we used only that makeup when we shot the girls. Ennui.

Daphne, of course, couldn't help but comment on my new low profile. She made a few disparaging remarks in that Daphne way, where it wasn't quite bitchy, more seemingly innocuous, but the undercurrent was harsh. One day when she ran into me in the bathroom she said, "Oh my God, there you are! I thought you fell down a well or something! You used to be omni and now you're like milk carton." I just laughed it off. Another day, when I got into the elevator at five, Daphne looked at her posse and said, "I wish I could leave early, but work is so intense in the ed-in-chi's office that I simply can't. You gals are so *lucky.*"

But what really bugged me was when Daphne pranced into the photo department one day when I was being subjected to a particularly embarrassing form of torture that befalls interns in the bookings office. The beauty department was doing a story called "Makeup Bag *Disasters!*" and they had forced me, along with some other low-level assistants, to dump out our cosmetic kits—without warning—and then a photographer immediately swooped in and took pictures while the editor criticized everything I had. ("*Ewwww!* That mascara must be like five years old?" she'd screamed, recoiling. "Do you get a lot of styes?" And then she picked up a smushed tampon and said, "You're not blocking anything with this puppy. Don't wear white pants!" I was humiliated.) I was thanking God that James was out of the office when I heard Daphne's aristocratic snotty voice behind me say, "I heard from a little birdy that you and Matt are splitsville. I am so sorry if you are having a Jenny Ani moment."

I just looked up at her and smiled, knowing revenge would come soon enough. "Yeah, he dumped me. I was really bummed, but he was out of my league in a way. I can't compete with all his private jets and flashy vacations."

It practically *killed* me that Daphne's eyes lit up with a sparkle, but I knew that I had to plant seeds in order to pay them both back. Daphne drove me nuts. *Little birdy?* Who says that? Who are these little birdies and can we please call pest control?

One night I had to stay late. CeCe was out in the Hamptons on vacation and kept calling me to change the model on the shoot the next morning. Her indecision was killing me. First she wanted an Icelandic beauty, then a Swiss Miss, and then an African Queen. I felt so guilty calling and booking these girls—seemingly giving them their first big shot—only to call back and cancel. Finally, at ten at night, the guy at the modeling agency said *enough,* that he would never let his big clients work with *Skirt* again if they kept jerking around his ingenues, and CeCe relented ("of course, he's bluffing; *everyone* wants to work with us, but I have a dinner, so fine"), and I was released.

As I was the last one there—even the maintenance crew had left—I walked alone down the darkened hallways toward the elevator. Most of the lights were out, except I noticed that the fashion closet was unlocked and the lights were on. That was odd. The editors were maniacs about closing up shop in the closet. All the stuff in there was worth, like, millions of dollars. Retail, anyway. There was fine jewelry, furs, designer clothes, shoes, everything. Maybe some editor was working late. I looked through the slit between the door and the wall and saw a shadowy figure trying on clothes. It was Cecilia.

"Hey," I said, popping into the closet.

Cecilia jumped as if she had seen a ghost.

"Oh my God, sorry to startle you!" I apologized. "I just thought I was the only one here."

"What are you doing here?" Cecilia snapped.

I was taken aback. "I had to finish something up for CeCe. What are *you* doing here?"

I glanced at the outfit she was wearing—a new Chanel suit that we had just gotten in—and then down at a pile of clothes that were stuffed into a T. Anthony suitcase with the monogrammed initials C.M.B. The closet was usually immaculate, so at first all I could think was that someone would be in deep doo-doo for leaving all those clothes scattered about. But then it all clicked, and I realized that the bag was Cecilia's and she was taking the clothes. Daphne had said someone was stealing from the closet, but she didn't know it was her *best friend*.

"I'm just helping clean up this closet," said Cecilia, pretending to be nonchalant. "Putting stuff away."

152

"Here, let me help you," I said, putting down my bag and moving to hang up the gorgeous Missoni dress that was draped on top of her bag.

"That's okay, I can do it," said Cecilia, somewhat testily.

"It's really no problem."

"Do you have to be little-miss-do-everything all the time, Kira? I mean, I know your boyfriend dumped you, but get a life."

I stepped back as if I had been slapped. Cecilia's perfectly sculpted nostrils were flaring and her eyes looked glazed.

"What are you talking about?" was all I could come up with.

"Just get lost. Go get a life or something and stop interfering. You're always trying to one-up everyone!"

That did it. "Cecilia, I would leave if I genuinely thought you were going to put these clothes back where they belong. But I have a feeling that you are going to steal them. I know we've had theft recently, and now I know it's you."

"Don't be ridiculous!" she said, her eyes ice.

It was a standoff, and a staredown.

"If I'm so ridiculous, then put the clothes back."

"You are so lame! You put them back," said Cecilia. She dumped the clothes out of her duffel. "I was just using my bag to gather the ones strewn around the room and then I was going to hang them up. But be my guest, Miss Goody Two-shoes."

She turned on her slingbacks and sauntered out. I stared at the mess she had made and, with a sigh, started to pick up the gorgeous handmade clothes one by one. Some of them were so beautiful that they were almost like artwork. I couldn't believe that Cecilia, someone who had everything, would steal. I know kleptomania is a disease and has nothing to do with what you do or don't have, but I think in her case it was more a case of spoiled-brat-itis. Nice friends, Daphne. Good job.

Chapter Twenty-Seven

I was unprepared for what went down the next day. I had taken the subway with Gabe and Teagan as usual, and we spent most of the time brainstorming and rehearsing Gabe's imminent confession to his parents. At first I didn't notice anything was amiss when we got upstairs (although the petrified look of our bug-eyed receptionist should have alerted me), and it wasn't until I got to CeCe's office that I noticed the hallways were unusually quiet. As soon as CeCe saw me, she quickly hung up the phone, pressed the intercom buzzer, and said, "She's here." Then she reknotted her Hermès scarf, which I'd seen her do when she was nervous, and came out from behind the desk, barring my entrance into her office.

"Genevieve wants to talk to you."

I was confused. Genevieve? The editor in chief? What was this about?

"Me?"

"Yes, you," said CeCe, her cigarette breath whipping my face.

"Okay," I said. "Should I, um, go to her office?"

CeCe nodded solemnly.

This was so odd. Did Cecilia confess and Genevieve want to ask me about it? Or was this about the job that Alida promised I would get? I couldn't imagine, but my mind raced. The way people looked at me when I walked by warned me that it wasn't going to be a pleasant conversation. I nervously straightened my long-sleeve button-down shirt that I had tucked into my black skirt with the side bow, and was glad I had gone conservative today. I was wearing nice silver ballerina flats and simple jewelry, and knew I had to pass muster.

When I entered Genevieve's outer office, her two assistants—who I had never seen smile—gave me a look and one of them nodded. "She's ready for you."

I walked through the glass door and saw Daphne sitting regally, legs crossed, on the first chocolate brown fauteuil. I glanced around the room and noticed Cecilia and Alida, who were both sitting on the sofa, and then turned my head to meet Genevieve's gaze. For someone so tiny—I mean, literally, the woman was no bigger than half an Olsen twin—she was an incredibly imposing presence. I watched her eyes study my outfit from head to toe, slowly, as if she had all the time in the world and this was super important, before she met my gaze. She stared at me for what seemed like a full minute before speaking.

"Kira, is it?"

"Yes," I said meekly. I felt like I was a model at a go-see.

"So, what's going on, Kira?" said Genevieve. She had the ability to speak without moving any other part of her body besides her lips. I usually talk with my hands, especially when I'm nervous, but she remained unmoved. No wonder she had burned up the corporate ladder. That was a skill.

"I guess I'm not sure what you mean," I said. I wanted to turn and look at Alida for support, but I would have had to contort my entire body to see her, and I figured that wasn't a good idea.

"Last night Cecilia saw you in the fashion closet stuffing clothes into your bag. Can you explain?" Genevieve said, again cool as a cucumber.

This could not be happening! Cecilia was blaming me?

"What? That is *not* what happened, Genevieve," I said, quivering. But then I tried to summon the power of my voice. Confident! Be confident! I reminded myself. "I was working late on a project for CeCe and when I left I noticed the light on in the closet and I saw Cecilia trying on clothes and putting them into *her* duffel bag."

"I knew she would do this!" said Cecilia loudly, slapping her hand on her thigh. I turned to glare at her.

"Don't worry. Genevieve knows the truth," said Daphne to Cecilia, reassuringly.

"It was a T. Anthony monogrammed duffel with Cecilia's initials," I said, as if this information proved my point.

"Genevieve, she's clearly lying," said Daphne smoothly. "Cecilia is a *Barney*. She has all the money in the world. There's no way she needs to steal anything. She has an entire shop filled with everything."

"Kleptomania has nothing to do with need," I said lamely. Oh my God! They all thought I did this.

"Alida?" asked Genevieve coolly.

I turned and looked at Alida imploringly. Please be my ally!

"I have to be honest, Kira has been the best intern I think we've ever had. She always works late and pitches in, and I've never seen her take anything for herself. It seems out of character."

Thank you, Alida! I smiled nervously at her.

"Of course, now it all makes sense *why* she worked late. She wanted the opportunity to take things," interjected Daphne. Bitch!

"Daphne, I don't even know where the key to the closet is," I said.

"That's a stupid excuse. You could have swiped it from someone," said Daphne, seething. We both glared at each other.

"Genevieve, you can come to my apartment and search everything. I promise you I didn't take anything. Cecilia, will you let them come over to your apartment and check your closets?" I asked, turning to her. I saw Cecilia squirm.

"Ridiculous! There's no reason to do that," said Daphne. "Kira probably already sold everything. There's a big black market for this stuff."

"I would totally let you over to look at my stuff, but because of who my parents are and the fact that we live on Park Avenue, there's all sorts of legal stuff that has to happen first," said Cecilia. Lame excuse.

"Someone's lying," said Genevieve evenly, glancing at me and then Cecilia.

"Not me!" Cecilia and I both said in unison.

"Kira, how did you come to us?" asked Genevieve, again motionless.

"She's a Cotton intern," Alida interjected. "She won the position over hundreds of qualified applicants."

"Where are you from?" asked Genevieve.

"Outside Philadelphia," I said.

"Hmmm . . ." said Genevieve. I could tell she was trying to process in her head how much money that meant I had. She was leaning toward me as the culprit!

Suddenly there was a knock on the door.

Everyone turned and saw James through the glass. He waved and Genevieve nodded to let him in.

"Sorry to interrupt, but I think I can clear this up," said James.

"Really . . ." said Genevieve, more as a statement than a question.

"Daphne told me about the theft a few weeks ago, so I put one of the cameras from the photo department in the closet, you know, to record who is there after hours. I think if we look at it, we can see who is really telling the truth," said James, glancing at me and winking.

Yaaay. My knight in shining armor! My hero! I whipped my head around and looked at Cecilia, who had now melted into the sofa. She looked nauseous.

"Does anyone want to say anything now?" asked Genevieve.

"Bring it on," I said confidently.

"Let's do it," said Daphne, standing up.

"Wait!" shouted Cecilia, holding out her arm to stop Daphne's departure for the screening.

Every head in the room whipped in her direction and could tell at once, from her guilty expression, what the outcome would be.

"Do you have something to say?" asked Genevieve, her tone unreadable.

"Okay, I was borrowing stuff from the closet, but I totally planned on giving it back. Daphne borrows all the time, and I just didn't think it was a big deal. Daphne even gave me a key," confessed Cecilia.

"*What?*" screamed Daphne. "That key was not to be used recreationally. That was in case of emergency, for me, because I always lose my keys." She addressed the last part to the entire room, but it fell flat.

"Alida, did you tell your interns that nothing was ever to be borrowed from the closet without permission?" asked Genevieve.

160

"Maybe one hundred times," said Alida.

"Come on, everyone borrows," insisted Cecilia.

"Not lately, not since the theft," I said. "And besides, we all know you weren't *borrowing*. When you borrow, you tell other people. You were stealing."

There was pin-drop silence as we all waited for Cecilia to respond. Finally she stood up and flipped her hair. "You know what? I don't want to deal with this. It's like a minor misunderstanding that you're making into a big tragedy. I don't need to work, and I don't need to stand here accused of stuff. I'm going to go talk to my lawyer."

Then she walked across the office, opened the door, and sauntered out.

Silence.

"Sorry, Kira!" said Alida, coming up and giving me a big hug.

Daphne looked confounded but quickly recovered. "How horrible this must have been for you!" she said, embracing me. "Cecilia had us all duped. Now we know her true colors! Let's have lunch and do a rehash and regroup. I'm so shaken."

"Um, raincheck maybe," I said. I turned and looked at Genevieve to await her response.

"Well, that's settled. I have a nine o'clock, so if you'll all excuse me," she said coolly.

I couldn't believe that was all she said, after my frigging life was on the line. But, whatever. I wanted to get the hell out of there and get this over with.

I left the office, arm in arm with Alida, but not before turning to James and thanking him. Profusely.

"No prob," he said with a wink.

God, he was hot.

Chapter Twenty-Eight

*A*fter an Oscar-worthy reenactment of the war zone that was Genevieve's office, I had Gabe and Teagan drooling. I thought Teagan would literally go out and bash in Cecilia's face with a polo mallet, but I mollified her with the parting image of the humiliated Trumpette leaving red-faced and stammering about her lawyers.

"Rock *on*, girlfriend!" exclaimed Gabe, high-fiving me dramatically. He saluted me so loudly that everyone sitting near us in the Lower East Side dive bar Crush turned around to see the owner of the larynx that had projected so far across the room.

And speaking of crushes: Not to be so 1950s, but something about James's saving my ass made me feel very much the damsel in distress who was rescued. Big time. But the still-lingering embarrassment over slumming with Matt clouded my confidence with him. When I'd spied James a couple times later in the day, he was busy bolting around and could barely spare a sec to chitchat. Gabe and Teagan looked at each other slyly as I described James's foresight and *Mission: Impossible*–style gadgetry with full unprompted camera installation.

"That's hot," Gabe agreed. "Almost as delish as Tom Cruise in that harness. Yummy."

"I mean, he totally helped me dodge a bullet," I mused aloud. "I could have been *arrested*, not just canned. I feel like I owe him majorly."

"Aren't you glad you saved the V-pass?" Gabe teased. Teagan snorted out her Diet Coke.

"Shut up!" I said, feeling my pale cheeks blush again.

"Oooooh! Kira and James sittin' in a tree—" Gabe sang.

"You guys, I'm serious—how do I thank him—not in a horizontal way, Gabe. He would *never* be into me in that way, anyway. . . ."

"Hmmm . . . What do you both love?" asked Teagan, hand on chin as she perused the pages of *Time Out New York*, the city's "obsessive guide to impulsive entertainment" with everything to do, eat, watch, and visit under the New York sun.

"How about buying him a cool photograph?" Gabe offered.

"Reminder: I'm broke," I offered.

"I got it!" Teagan said, wide-eyed. "Check it out! Look at this ad. In teeny letters it says the Damguards are playing Monday at The Mercury Lounge!"

Gabe and I looked at each other. I suddenly felt very uncool to ask my next question.

"Who are they?" I asked sheepishly. "I've never heard of them."

Teagan laughed. "Kira, it's Radiohead. They do sneak shows under a code name for die-hard fans. James would die and go to heaven," she said, eyes ablaze. "And the tickets are el-cheapo 'cause it's at such a tiny venue that the ticket cartels can't screw you. It's perfect!"

As the corners of my mouth turned up for a smile, I heard the group's music in my head. I couldn't think of a better thank-you-for-saving-my-hide present.

"A surprise?" James asked, cocking his head to one side. "What kind of surprise?"

"How could I tell you? It would ruin it," I said knowingly. The tickets were burning a hole in my pocket, and I could not have been more revved up.

"You don't have to do anything for me, Kira. The only reward I need is the sweet taste of justice," he said with a laugh.

"Well, Spider-Man, that's very bold, but I still feel the need to

165

thank you, so Monday night consider yourself booked."

One thing I did know as he waved good-bye to enter his staff meeting: The crush from June that had withered on the vine was now back in bloom.

uckily I didn't have too much time during the weekend to dwell on my impending sorta-date (at least in my mind) with James because Gabe's parents had come to town and it was time for a Dr. Phil–style sit-down. I was nauseous for him, but I was also nauseous for myself and Teagan because Gabe insisted that we be there to serve as cheerleaders. It seemed totally inappropriate for me to be caught in the middle of a major family revelation, but Gabe said he really needed our strength and support to get through it.

It's funny, because the way I had envisioned his parents was nothing like the reality. Yes, okay, I subscribe to stereotypes (guilty!), but instead of a plump, frosted-blonde, matronly midwestern woman clad in Talbots, Gabe's mother was petite and totally chic with her Sally Hershberger–style tousled haircut, Bottega Veneta handbag, and miniskirt. I suppose due to Gabe's description I had expected his father to come into the apartment toting a football and clad in all sorts of University of Wisconsin paraphernalia, but instead the guy was wearing a fairly innocuous Lacoste shirt and jeans.

And they were nice. I mean, super nice. Which makes sense because Gabe was super nice. But I had pictured characters from *Desperate Housewives* ready to do all sorts of evil deeds from Gabe's description. It's not like he bashed them—I guess his giant fear about telling them he was gay made me think they'd be satanic.

"It is so nice to finally meet you," said Gabe's mom ("Call me Meg!"), who greeted me with a kiss.

Gabe's father, Mitch, was less affectionate but pumped my hand several times with enthusiasm.

"Can we get you anything to drink?" asked Teagan.

"We bought champagne at that cute store on the corner!" said Meg. "We wanted to have a celebration."

"Thanks for looking after our boy," said Mitch. "His mother was so worried sending him off to the big bad city."

"You're embarrassing him," said Meg, tousling Gabe's hair. He indeed looked embarrassed.

"Shall I open it?" asked Mitch, pulling the champagne out of a paper bag.

After pouring the drinks and chitchatting for a while, Gabe's parents started to throw out a few feelers about going back to their hotel to shower before dinner. Teagan and I nervously glanced at Gabe, wondering if he would go through with it. It was starting to look like he might bail out, but we knew that we couldn't let him.

"So, Mitch, Meg, are your other children living close to home?" asked Teagan, giving Gabe a look.

"Yes, we're so lucky. Mary-Elizabeth is married with two children, lives just down the street, and Patricia teaches second grade at Sacred Heart; Chad is a senior at Madison. He wants to be a physical therapist, or maybe do something with sports medicine, that's his passion, and J.P. will be a sophomore, as obsessed with football as the rest of my boys. Well, except Gabe."

"We were surprised Gabe even worked at *Sports Today*," said Mitch.

"I don't," Gabe blurted out.

He had been so silent that his words took everyone by surprise.

"What do you mean?" asked Meg, confused.

Teagan and I watched as he shot us a look before taking a slow, deep breath. "I told you I was working there but I'm not. I work at *Skirt* magazine. You know, the fashion magazine."

His parents paused. "Why wouldn't you tell us that?" asked Mitch, perplexed.

"Maybe we should go," I said, rising.

"Please stay," pleaded Gabe.

I felt so awkward in the middle of the Jerry Springer moment but I had to honor my friend's wishes.

"Mom, Dad, I'm gay," said Gabe, finally looking at his parents.

I stared at them, waiting for the screams and the cries, but they didn't say anything. Gabe spoke again.

"And I'm going to the Parsons School of Design, which is a fashion school, because I want to be a designer, not a football player."

Meg seemed to inhale slowly, and then she looked at Mitch, whose face I couldn't read.

You could cut the tension with a seam ripper.

"Sweetie, we're so happy for you," said Meg.

I was stunned. *What?* Did she just say, "happy for him"?

Gabe looked up at her. "You are?"

"Sweetie, your father and I had sort of thought for a long time that you might be, you know, gay, but we didn't think you knew it, so we didn't want to say anything."

"We went to a therapist, you know, at, what's it called, Meggie?"

"Gay and Lesbian Support Network," said Meg, nodding.

"Right," said Mitch. "And we asked them what to do—you know, we think our son is gay and he doesn't know it. . . ."

"And they said not to do anything, that you'll figure it out in your own time," interjected Meg.

"But we were worried that you had your heart set on football at Madison, wanted to follow in your big brother's footsteps, and maybe that wouldn't be the right place for you and you'd get frustrated," said Mitch softly.

Suddenly Gabe burst into tears. Heaving, sobbing tears. His mother went to him and gave him a big giant hug.

"So you're not mad at me?" asked Gabe.

"Of course not, sweetie," said Meg. "We want you to be happy."

"What about you, Dad?" asked Gabe.

"I'm not used to it, I admit. But I know it's genetic, it can't be helped, and it's who you are, and I love who you are. Jesus tells us to love everyone without judgment," said Mitch.

"Oh my God! I should have told you *years* ago!" said Gabe, still crying but also laughing.

Tears were streaming down my cheeks also. And I stole a glance at the impenetrable Teagan, who was also sobbing.

"But honey, I think you need to apply to Parsons," said Meg gently.

"I did. I'm in!" said Gabe.

"Well, then this calls for a celebration!" said his father, pouring more champagne.

We spent the next hour laughing and crying while Gabe filled in his parents on his summer at *Skirt* and how nervous he was about telling them and everything else. Finally Gabe and his parents left for dinner, and Teagan and I, emotionally wrecked from the day's events, rented *The Princess Bride* and ordered in Chinese before retiring to bed at ten o'clock. If only everything had happy endings like that.

Chapter Thirty

*A*fter a night of full MSG binging, I returned to work, ready to begin my final two weeks as a summer intern at *Skirt*. While Gabe was having a good-bye breakfast with his parents, Teagan and I boarded the packed Hughes elevators as usual.

But when they opened on our floor, the mood was most certainly out of the ordinary. A pall had been cast over the normally bustling office. As I was having acid flashbacks of Charlie Sheen's final scene in *Wall Street* when he meandered through the maze of cubicles, I noticed not one but two grim-faced staffers carrying boxes of belongings. Teagan and I looked at each other as if to say *huh?* And then we saw Richard.

"Girls! In here!" he whispered. We obediently darted into the conference room.

He was fanning himself with our last issue, sweating. "You're gonna *die!*" he exclaimed breathlessly. "Heads are rolling!"

"What's going on?" Teagan asked.

"Over the weekend, we all got calls for an emergency staff meeting at eight A.M. this morning. We haven't had that since Genevieve's predecessor, Miranda DuChoix, was fired on Saturday's Page Six in the *Post!*" he said, eyes ablaze. "So we all gather around this morning, and who shows up but Mr. Hughes, who said he sold the magazine to Sly Oldshack after an offer even he couldn't refuse!"

No. Way. We were too stunned to respond. The rug had been totally ripped out from the staff's Louboutin-covered feet—not a soul knew about the sale and the whole crew was totally blindsided.

"And get this: Genevieve's out," whispered Richard. "Alida's in. She's the new editor in chief! Apparently, she's been having secret meetings for months with Sly Oldshack, presenting her ideas."

Suddenly Richard's words triggered the memory of seeing Alida in that out-of-the-way restaurant. So *that* was who I saw Alida with that time near the studio! It wasn't a secret affair behind her boyfriend's back; it was a clandestine job meeting behind Genevieve's back!

"Oh my God!" Teagan squealed giddily. I loved how my Goth comrade was suddenly alive with the spark of scandal.

"First order of bidniss," said Richard, looking both ways. "Firings galore. CeCe was the first to get canned. She called Alida a bitch and stormed out!"

My jaw hit the table. So there was justice in the world.

"Half the staff is Audi 5000," he said, listing the sackings, which obviously included the dispatching of Daphne to *Tinsel Monthly*, which Daddy still owned. "But luckily you are looking at the nuevo senior editor!"

Teagan and I jumped up and hugged him, but our congratulatory embrace was interrupted by a rapping on the conference room window. Oops, busted. We turned to find Alida herself looking in. She signaled to me to come outside. Uh oh, was I in trouble? Maybe I shouldn't have been so publicly gleeful when there was a job guillotine snapping down on half the editors' skinny necks.

I followed her outside into the hallway, gulping.

"So, Kira," she said, smiling calmly. "I know you start Columbia this fall—"

"Mmm-hmm," I responded, wondering why she wanted to talk to me.

"So it's a good thing our new offices are on the Upper West Side," she said, eyebrow arched as she smiled, awaiting my response—which was simply utter confusion.

"What do you mean?" I probed.

Alida laughed and put a hand on my shoulder. "What I mean," she said, "is that you were one of the best interns I have ever seen in my tenure here. You have your ear to the ground, you're a killer trendspotter, you have guts, soul, and"—she looked me in the eye—"heart."

I didn't know what to say.

"I want you on our team," she said, to my disbelief. "We need a girl on the street, a college editor. I want you to helm your own section of the magazine, like a hip shopper's index in the back of the book. You're dedicated, chic, and I know you have a really bright future in this business. You think you can handle it on top of schoolwork?"

Yes! Yes! A thousand times yes! "Alida, I'd be *honored*!" I gushed, hand on heart. It was literally the greatest thing that could happen. And screw stamping books in the library or some menial go-nowhere job, the *Skirt* money would help fund my student life and be a humongous resume builder! I was reeling.

"All along I watched you work late, stay focused, and even deal with Daphne with total grace," she said. "It wasn't fair. And life's not fair. But your work did not go unnoticed. I for one was very impressed. And your diligence and perseverance really reminded me of someone," she said with a grin.

"Who?" I asked.

"Me."

I only hoped my future would be half as major, as Alida would now flank the front of every runway from here to Milan. Instead of being cold and demanding, she was a true leader who would actually teach her staff instead of berate them.

"I can't thank you enough," I said, hugging her. "This is literally my dream come true!"

And it was. And now there was only one more reverie left to conquer.

Chapter Thirty-One

"Ready?"

I turned around and saw James leaning against the wall by the door. He looked H.O.T. in his white T-shirt, khakis, and scuffed-up Vans—so hot that I had to exhale slowly and tell myself to keep it together. Sometimes simple is best. More people should understand that. Maybe that would be my first column, called "Miniskirt," for the new *Skirt*. My mind was meandering because I was nervous.

"Sure," I said. "Let me just get my stuff."

I grabbed my bag and felt myself blush for no apparent reason. It was odd. I see James day in, day out, but it was like there was this new shift; we were both swingin' single and now he could potentially be *mine*. I could be on an episode of *Maury*: "When Friends Become Lovers." Although I was getting ahead of myself.

We barely spoke to each other as we exited the office because there were so many people around, so it wasn't until we got in the taxi (I was planning on taking the subway but James wanted to splurge) that we had a chance to chat.

"Congratulations on your new gig," I said to James. Alida had made him senior photo editor.

"To you as well," said James.

The leather seats felt hot on the back of my legs, and I just prayed when we got out that I wouldn't have all those weird markings and red lines smashed on my thighs. Maybe it was a bad idea to wear a short frock.

"Cute dress," said James. I blushed, but then realized he must have seen me adjust it over and over again.

"Thanks."

Why was I so mute and fidgety? I was acting like a mime in Central Park. So much had transpired but I didn't know what to say.

"And thanks again for, you know, saving me the other day. It was just my luck that you had cameras in there and caught Cecilia on tape."

"I have a confession to make," said James with a smile. "I didn't have cameras in there," he said. "I was bluffing."

Shock. "What?"

James crossed his ankles, put his hands behind his head, and stretched like a cat who'd just chowed a canary. "I knew you didn't steal, and I knew that you'd go down for it, and I couldn't let that happen."

My mind raced. "James, what, what if they called you on it?" I sputtered.

"I kind of didn't have that part covered. But I knew I had to do something, and it was the first thing that came to mind."

His unflinching gaze suddenly made me bold. "Why did you know you had to do something?" I asked coyly.

James looked at me, cocked his head to the side, and then smiled again. "Because I like you, Kira."

Before I could talk myself into a bumbling lather, James leaned in and kissed me. His lips were soft, and he slowly put his arms around my waist so that I felt myself falling backward into the leather backseat. It had been nice with Matt, but something now just clicked and I knew that this was what it was supposed to feel like. It was all tingly and strange and too good to be true. We kissed the entire way downtown; the beeps and honks and sirens of New York seemed to fade to mute as we kissed deeper and deeper, almost as if we were making up for lost time. The whole summer, we were meters apart down the hall but miles apart in terms of being at this moment. Better late than never.

When we got to the venue and I revealed my surprise, his jaw hit the floor as he pulled me into him.

"Kira Parker. I can't believe you!"

I could tell he was overjoyed by my secretly hatched plan and euphoric at the rush of the music starting—as I myself was on cloud nine thousand just to be beside him. Radiohead's songs made everything that much more explosive as we made out under the blue-hued lights, but the truth was, we could have had a soundtrack of cacophonous sirens and it would have felt like Eden in that sweaty concert hall. We kissed nonstop throughout the set (we must have looked like those annoying people that you tell to get a room) and continued at the bar we went to after. It wasn't until after James had walked me home and I floated to bed that I realized what this feeling was—I was in love.

I always love a good update, so let me just press the fast-forward button and tell you where things ended up six months after our cab mack-fest. The taxi home crashed into a wall, leaving us on side-by-side respirators at New York Hospital. Just kidding. Seriously, it could not have turned out better: After Alida's premier issue of *Skirt*, newsstand sales soared. The new team was so passionate and dedicated and the whole vibe of the office was refreshed and excited. Alida led the staff in a great way—instead of being scared of our boss, we all looked up to her and wanted to do our best to kick ass. The mag was already nominated for multiple awards and had a cool new look and fun feel; people were reading it cover to cover, including my column, which I am thrilled to say has gotten great feedback through reader mail.

One day, while I had my nose in magazine spreads, a smiling Alida plopped a tabloid in my face. The *New York Post* featured a huge article with the headline HUGHES PUB HEIRESS SWINDLED. It went on to say that Daphne Hughes's boyfriend, Matt, who had several aliases, had charged up a storm on her credit card and her daddy's various accounts about town. She and pops would be pressing full charges, and her humiliation was as public as it gets. I kind of felt bad for her. But not that bad. As for "Matt," he faced up to three years in the slammer. Karma!

When school started in September, I made a concerted effort to really be engaged, not just for my role at the magazine, but also for myself. I've managed to build a student life at Columbia— I have great new friends, I worship my professors, and I truly feel immersed in campus culture. But when the gang hits the keggers or has dorm room fiestas, I can push the eject button I'd made for myself over the summer. Instead of grody cafeteria food, I meet up with Gabe and Teagan (who are both loving their programs) for yummy ethnic binges downtown. When my roommate goes to scream at football games, I am working a Saturday shift at *Skirt* or wandering the streets finding cool boutiques opened by young designers in Brooklyn.

The cute frat boys my pals pine over may be great, but as I do my math problem sets or art history essays in the library, I don't get distracted by them. Because I know when I am done, James will pick me up for another New York adventure—bands, photo shoots, late dinners, or just long walks. Last week, Alida told me that the fall collections (always shown the season before on the European runways) would be smack in the middle of my spring break from school, so I would be going on my first-ever trend-spotting trip with the senior fashion editors. James scheduled a huge cover shoot with the model du jour at the same time, so we'll be together in the City of Light. I can't believe it; I feel so lucky that I stayed on my own path all summer, which led me to now: the once-miserable summer intern who ended up the happiest girl in the Big Apple.